A Life in Progress

a novel

by

Michelle Fornelli

Copyright © 2023 by Michelle Fornelli

All rights reserved. No part of this publication may be reproduced, distributed, or transmitted in any form or by any means, including photocopying, recording or other electronic or mechanical methods, without the prior written permission of the author, except in the case of brief quotations embodied in reviews and certain other non-commercial uses permitted by copyright law.

This is a work of fiction. Any characters, businesses, places, events, and incidents are either the products of the author's imagination or used in a fictitious manner. Any resemblance to actual persons, living or dead, or actual events is purely coincidental.

Printed in the United States of America

Hardcover ISBN: 978-1-959096-66-5
Paperback ISBN: 978-1-959096-67-2
Ebook ISBN: 978-1-959096-68-9

**Canoe Tree
Press**

4697 Main Street
Manchester Center, VT 05255

Canoe Tree Press is a division of DartFrog Books

"What lies behind us and what lies before us are tiny matters compared to what lies within us."

—Ralph Waldo Emerson

DEDICATION

For my husband—who always believes
in me and is my beacon of light.

To my parents and siblings—for always
being there for me.

For all the people out there searching for
dreams. Keep searching—just don't give up.

CHAPTER 1

It is mid-October, and a steady rain is pounding on the tin roof so loud I cannot even hear myself think. It sounds as if a band of steel drums is playing outside my bedroom window, and I am listening in on the party.

I love this time of year. As the weather cools, the leaves begin making their grand appearance, like all the years before, displaying their beautiful, brilliant colors. Reds, oranges, browns, and yellows speckle the trees like dabs of fresh paint on an artist's canvas. The landscape is so overcome with the autumnal display it is hard not to appreciate the beauty of the season. Ever since I was a kid, something in the richness of the season just before winter sets in has given me comfort so strong it is like a blanket wrapping around me. I cannot imagine living someplace that does not partake in this magical change of seasons.

It is still early. The sun has not come up yet, but I already know what time it is. Like clockwork, Luigi silently sticks his wet nose up to the top of the bed, tail wagging. He is always so happy to see me. He is ready to go out. I can hear him getting restless on the floor next to the bed, and I am biding my time to see how long he will wait for me. Dogs never seem to mind the temperature outside, blinding rain, or blowing snow. They have one mission, and that is *out.* I roll over to my right side and pat him, draping my left hand across his head. At nearly ninety pounds and still growing, Luigi is a Great Pyrenees mix and the most beautiful pup in the world. His coat is a cream color with dabs of tan on his big paws. A white stripe runs from the top of his furry head to the start of his nose and a sprinkling of black freckles on his long snout. The black diamond-shaped patches around his eyes make him look like a child playing with makeup, putting black eyeshadow everywhere it is not supposed to be. Most of all, I adore his floppy, frizzy ears. I fell in love with him the moment we saw him at the rescue over a year ago. All the dogs were waiting for some love and attention, eager for the first person to make their acquaintance. It was hard to imagine how anyone could have abandoned them.

"Five more minutes," I plead. "Just five more minutes." I don't have to get up. I have nowhere to go. If not for Luigi, I probably would not get up for another several hours.

I lost my job as a bank teller about three months ago. Not that I ever loved it. I did not mind it. The people at the bank were nice. I had a lot of friends there, and since it was a small town, most of the customers were regulars and I knew them all by name. They came in routinely to make withdrawals and deposit checks, and sometimes I think the older customers came in for the conversation. While they would never have said so, I think they were lonely. They seemed so happy to have a few moments of interaction with another human being. Regardless of the reasons, it was always nice to know I helped in some small way. Being in a small town has its perks. People are not in a rush and small towns have a big way of making you feel important. The bank gave me a reason to get up in the morning and earn a paycheck. To have a purpose and to be needed: those two things are vital to living, I think.

I was not the only one who lost a job, however. The bank closed. It had not been doing well for years and we could all see the writing on the wall. Even though the closure had been expected, it was still a shock when the bank shut its doors for the last time. I think everyone was surprised and sad that we would not be spending our days together anymore, as we had for fifteen years. The last day was exceptionally hard. Most of us knew we probably would not see each other again unless we made an effort. The bank was one of the few places in town that drew workers from far away. We all left that day promising to get together, but many had kids or other family members to care for. We knew it would be highly unlikely. Still, the thought was there.

I always used to like getting up early. Lately, though, getting up seems to take all my strength. My husband wakes up hours before sunrise, and I feel guilty sleeping in when I know he is hard at work, even though he never complains. At the end of the day, I find relief in going to bed earlier and earlier. I can drown out my thoughts and not have to think of anyone or anything. I do not have to explain why I always feel so bad. I can simply fall into the bliss of the unknown and escape the realities of my day. People never seem to understand anyway. They see things how they want to see them, and no amount of explaining can make them understand the gravity of my situation. I know I am not alone, but feeling this way keeps me isolated and realizing that makes me feel even worse. At least for several hours of uninterrupted sleep, I can let my thoughts drift away.

Now I can see daylight coming in around the edges of the blackout Roman shades hanging on the window beside me. Even though I want to bury myself farther under the pillow and let my body melt into the bed, Luigi pokes his head up once more, thinking I have forgotten about him. His puppy-dog eyes have an almost human quality as he looks eagerly at me, willing me to play with him and let him out. As I reluctantly push back the blush-colored paisley duvet, a blast of cold air washes over me, and I shiver. We have not turned the furnace on yet. Every year it is like a game to see how long we can go before we have to turn on the heat. This is going to be the day. I sit up on the bed, lower my feet over the edge, and rest my heels on the frame of the walnut sleigh bed as I search for my favorite pink fluffy slippers. They are so worn that the stuffing is falling out of the sides, but I cannot bring myself to buy new ones. They were a gift from my husband a few Christmases ago. "They're so *you*," Gino said, and he was right. They have cute little bows on the heels with a sparkly gem in the center of each bow. I love wearing things that sparkle. It is like an all-day celebration; it makes me happy. I know eventually I will succumb and replace the pink fluffy slippers, but I will hang onto them for as long as I can. I tend to be sentimental about gifts. Knowing that someone took the time to gift me something makes my possessions more special. That I was worthy of someone's thoughtfulness makes me feel less ordinary.

I see my slippers peeking out from under the bed, and I step down and slip my feet into them. They envelop my feet like warm pockets. Nearby hangs my pink terry-cloth robe with a bow and sparkling gem on the right lapel to match the slippers. I wrap myself in the robe and squat to give Luigi his first belly rub of the day. His happiness is contagious, and as I let out a laugh, he rolls on his back and slowly extends first one paw into the air, followed by the other. He looks as if he is raising his hands to ask a question. I ask him what his question is, but he is so content with the belly rubs that his head falls to the side. He looks so blissfully happy.

As I stand up, Luigi rolls over and gets up too. He follows me to the door and through the long hallway. As I make my way down the wooden plank stairs, each step singing a song, I hear the click of Luigi's claws on the wood floor.

I walk into the kitchen and sitting on the center of the island countertop is the most beautiful bouquet of roses I have ever seen. These are not just any roses. They are "I love you more than anything in the world" roses. They are crimson with velvety petals so lush and silky that looking at them makes me feel beautiful. While I have never considered myself pretty, let alone beautiful, my husband has always made me feel I am. I am not what one would call heavy, but I am not exactly petite. My athletic five-foot-six frame has always hidden my pockets of unwanted weight. I try to stay in shape, but it is often a challenge, especially now, when all I want to do is curl up in bed all day. My shoulder-length mousy-brown hair is often pulled into a ponytail—mostly to keep it out of my face but also because it is the easiest style to produce, and I can look as if I have attempted to put some effort into it. Next to my husband, whose Italian background gave him beautifully tan skin, I look pale. My skin burns at the first dose of summer sun. While I loved the outdoors growing up, my friends often laughed at me for always covering my face with hats and sunblock. I still do that, and I am thankful I stayed true to myself, because my skin has thanked me countless times by staying smooth and wrinkle-free, even now that I am closing in on forty.

Lying on the counter next to the vase is a small, folded card with my name written on the cover in my husband's handwriting. *Francesca.* Smiling, I think about how I love hearing him say my full name. Often he calls me Fran, but on the occasions when he calls me by my full name, it seems to roll off his tongue so eloquently. He has lived in America longer than in Italy, but every now and then, I can detect a slight accent in how he says certain words. I pick up the card and open it. It reads, *"I wanted you to know that I'm thinking of you as I do every day. I love you. Love, Gino. P.S. We will get through this."* My heart explodes at my undying love for him. "We will get through this," he wrote. *We.* He knows. We have been married for fifteen years. I know he can read me like a book.

Standing in the kitchen with the card still in my hand, I am pulled out of my reverie by the sound of Luigi pacing at the back door to be let out. "Hold on. I'm coming," I say. I open the glass door, and before I can get the screen door even halfway open, he bolts outside, mindless of the pouring rain. I close both doors to keep the rain from coming in. Standing at the door, waiting for Luigi to come back, I stare at the rain and consider my plan for the day. I would like to go back to bed, which I seriously thought about, but then I thought of Gino. "No, I need to make myself productive," I tell myself. "Besides, I can't tell him I slept all day." I have two things in my corner: Gino and Luigi.

I am not skilled at hiding my feelings. Maybe I never learned how. I was never one of those kids who knew what I wanted to do with my life. I believed whatever I chose to do that I would be successful. The idea of failing or not becoming anything was inconceivable. When I was younger, ideas constantly flooded my head. I had dreams bigger than the stars and a belly full of nervous excitement. I was so full of hope and possibilities that I could explode. It was like the excitement I felt waking up on Christmas morning. I could not wait to grow up and be something or someone. "The world is a big place," someone told me once, "and there is a spot for everyone. Don't rush it, and things will fall into place." I genuinely believed that anything is possible. Yet here I am, grown up and still waiting to find my spot. I wish I could find what makes me happy. Why am I always so frustrated with myself? Why do I always feel lost in this big, beautiful world where I should be able to do anything or be anything? I know people do not understand. Living with this constant thought, I have difficulty understanding it myself.

I sit at the kitchen counter, looking at the vase of roses. I am so lucky. I have a loving and caring husband. I live in a good house. I drive a nice car. My husband has a great job that he loves. We are okay financially. I do not have to worry about that, for which I'm thankful. And my husband wants me to be happy with whatever I choose to do. So why am I unhappy? I have everything I could want. Why do I want more? I need to feel fulfilled. I need a sense of purpose and a reason to wake up in the morning. I need to find the one thing no one can help me with: my inner happiness. I do not know how to start looking for it. I mumble, "Why can't I be normal and happy with what I have? Why is it so difficult to find my place in this life?" Everyone tries to give me ideas and suggestions, but in the end, I am left with this dreadful feeling of doom that no amount of outside help can take away. It is exhausting.

I bury my head in my hands. I can feel the tears starting to stream down my face. I am trying so hard not to let these feelings overwhelm me, but they are all I can think about. To an onlooker, it would seem obvious. I imagine someone saying, "Get off your butt and make something happen!" I tell myself that every day, yet I feel like I cannot take my own advice. It is as if I'm in quicksand. The sand is so heavy on my body I can barely keep my head above the surface. Desperately grasping for one last gulp of air, I pray to God that he hears my prayers.

Will he? Is it my fate in this life to be in constant struggle? Is this my cross to bear? Thinking about it, I cannot help but feel remorseful. Some would laugh and say that this inner struggle is pure selfishness and I need to move on, get another job, and deal with it. I tell myself repeatedly that the internal pain I feel is nothing compared to the suffering of all the people in this world whose circumstances are more dire. How do I have the right to feel this way? But my pain and struggle are so immensely present that there are times I feel as if I physically cannot breathe. The wound is not visible, so outsiders never understand the degree of constant agony. It would almost be better to have a physical injury. At least then, people could imagine my pain instead of pretending it does not exist. Looking back, I think my mind has always been my worst enemy. It convinces me that I am not strong enough, not good enough, or not smart enough. Tragically, the human mind is so powerful that it can interfere with its ability to function.

Knowing there are people who are worse off than I am makes me feel more guilty. Yet I cannot seem to change anything.

Praying for hope, inspiration, or direction has become a daily ritual. My faith has always been a big part of my life, but so many moments have tested it. Yet I always direct my questions back to God. I keep telling myself that this path I am on has a purpose. I wish I knew what it is.

Suddenly I hear Luigi scratching at the door, and I get up from the table and let him in. His fur is so matted from the rain that he looks like he just climbed out of the pool. I try to grab his towel and throw it over him before he has a chance to shake himself dry, but I am too late. Water flies everywhere. Luigi runs around the kitchen, leaving a trail of muddy pawprints. I catch up and wrestle him between my knees to keep him from sprinting away while I clean off his paws. Satisfied with my attempt, he bolts out of the room and does his usual running lap around the house.

Exhausted, I fill Luigi's bowl, and rather than think about anything else, I go back to bed.

CHAPTER 2

Gino and I have a fairytale love story. We met the summer after I graduated from college. I was in Italy with some friends celebrating our final summer of relative freedom before we would hunker down into jobs and our real lives as mature, hardworking adults. Our group was tight-knit, but with everyone going their separate ways, we knew we probably would never get another chance to travel together.

About two days before the end of our Italian vacation, we ended up in Portofino, a fishing village on the coast near Genoa. We had no specific plans; we had all decided to spend our last few days in Italy however we wanted, meeting up in the evening for dinners. We were all going nonstop, so a leisurely day alone felt divine. I certainly enjoy the company of others, but I appreciate my alone time. It is my chance to recharge my thoughts and decompress.

It felt momentous to set out by myself, especially in a foreign country. Up to this point in our trip, the gang had all stuck together, but now, for the first time, I had the opportunity to prove to myself that I could venture out independently. I had the freedom to explore, and that won out over my fear of going solo.

Without any specific plan, I ventured out to see the beautiful village and explore all the artistic talent so readily visible on all the windowsills, market carts, and shops. And I did. I found stunning selections of silk scarves with deep, vibrant colors of oranges, blues, and greens. I couldn't decide on which colors to purchase, so in the end, I bought one of each to bring back to my friends and family. I found beautiful handmade cashmere wraps that I knew would work perfectly for the cooler evenings as well as a uniquely designed necklace with a thick gold chain and a mother of pearl teardrop stone the size of a lemon. Looking at the delicate pieces of glass and woodwork, I pretended I was an artist in training, carefully inspecting and admiring the works of many talented artists as if they had left their work out for me to study. It felt freeing and fun, but if I had told anyone I knew, they would have laughed heartily because I have no artistic skill. My love of music ends at my desire to listen to it. My love of books ends at my aptitude for reading them and getting lost in a world of my choosing. And my love of painting ends at my knack for appreciating high-quality art rather than perfecting beautiful brushstrokes on canvas. However, I love looking at art and recognize skill when I see it.

Fully satisfied in my search for artistic talent and having made a few selective purchases here and there, I decided to find a café. One of my favorite pastimes while traveling is to find someplace where I can sit outside and enjoy the beautiful scenes of local everyday life playing out before me. Browsing at the local vendors and enjoying the scene of people playing out before me, I had no idea I was walking up a hill. Shortly I came upon a café that overlooked the picturesque landscape of the village. It was a beautiful sight to take in—hotels built onto the sides of the cliffs with pops of color. Fishing boats filled with netting piled on the sides docked next to yachts of all sizes. And the smell—the air was permeated by the smell of baked bread with the added aroma of seawater. I sat and pulled a map from my well-worn crossbody leather bag pocket.

As I looked around at the occupied tables near me, I saw people animated and full of life. Everyone had a purpose. Those in conversations were fully engaged in either listening or speaking to their companions. Those sitting alone were either studying their surroundings or engrossed in the pages of a book. Both scenes were rarely observed stateside, even back then. Today, now that we have smartphones, I think most Americans are obsessed with their phones, even in the presence of others. It is as if we are afraid to enjoy our solitude for fear of what others may think. We also have an obsessive desire to constantly be in the know and in contact with people. We have lost the simple ability to be present, share in conversation, or observe and wonder at our surroundings. I think many Europeans still appreciate those gifts, but it is also easy to see that the passage of time is slowly erasing the simplicity enjoyed by past generations. People everywhere are moving faster, and even the places known for their usual languid lifestyles are slowly surrendering to the velocity of the transformation.

Flattening my map on the marble top of the café table, I pored over it, trying to figure out where I was. I heard a deep husky voice say, *"Scuzi. Si e perso. Come posso aiutarla?"* (Excuse me. You look lost. Can I help you?) Other than "Excuse me," I hadn't understood a word he said, so I waved him off with a friendly shake of my head, barely looking up from my map.

As I turned around to say, *"Io non parlo Italiano"* (I don't speak Italian), my heart caught, and I found myself staring into the eyes of a tall, incredibly handsome man about my age. His hair was a rich dark chestnut color, but I could tell he spent most of his time outdoors, given the mussed, sun-bleached strands around his face. His hair reached almost to his shoulders. He seemed completely unaware of his striking features, which made him even more attractive. At just over six feet, he bent down to look at the map.

"Can I help you?" he said.

"Oh, you speak English. Yes. No. Well, I am looking to see where I am and where I want to go. Can you show me where we are on the map?"

"We are in this spot right here," he said as he took his long index finger and positioned it at a spot on the map. "It is a good location. We are central to everything. There is no one thing you should see here, but simply enjoy everything you see. We are very visual, and everything is full of color and vibrancy. The sea, the shops, the restaurants, the homes, the art—even the music has color in it if you listen carefully."

"You speak English perfectly," I said. "I barely detect an accent. Are you from here?"

"Yes, originally, I am from here, but I live in New Jersey now," he replied.

"Well, *that* I didn't expect."

"May I join you for a coffee?" he asked. Not having any specific plans, I pushed out the chair next to me with my left foot and gestured to him with my hands. It felt nice to have some new company, and I wanted to hear a different perspective from someone who was not entirely a tourist. In a sense, I wanted to slip away and pretend that I was someone else living a carefree life, unlike mine. I had always been structured and organized. Spontaneous was not me. But being in the now and feeling empowered, I wanted to live for the moment. I was young and had the whole world in front of me, and I wanted to drink it all up.

We sat at the café for hours talking. I arrived just after three in the afternoon. The sun was shining bright, fishing boats were sailing in and out of the harbor, and the common spaces were filled with people fishing, eating, drinking, and sunbathing. Families walked hand in hand, kids ran around playing chase, lovers kissed, and friends walked and talked. These simple and unpretentious scenes of human interaction moved me: these are the moments life is made of. But now, the sun was coming in at a low angle, creating that sparkling effect on the water just before sunset, and signs of evening approached us from all around.

"We've been sitting here for hours," I said. "Weren't you on your way somewhere? Didn't you have any plans for this afternoon?" I picked up a fork and snagged a bite of the tiramisu a waiter brought to our table for us to share.

"Nothing that I can't do tomorrow. When you can enjoy the company of a beautiful woman, you take it," he said. He smiled proudly at me—a true Italian. Taking in every word he said, I analyzed them in every possible way. *He just called me beautiful,* I thought. At that moment, the whole world stopped around me. I had never been called beautiful by anyone before, let alone by a man this handsome.

Inside, I was reeling, but I casually glanced at my watch. That was when I realized I was over two hours late for dinner with my friends. I did not want the moment to end, but I knew my friends were probably worried sick about me. I quickly grabbed my leather bag off the back of the bistro chair and said I had to go.

"Wait," he said. "Can I see you again? We have a connection, you and I. It's not often you meet someone where you have an instant bond."

"It's been a wonderful afternoon. I enjoyed talking with you, but I am leaving in a few days." As I zig-zagged around the café tables and chairs, I called back to him. "Maybe I will see you tomorrow if it is meant to be."

On my way back to the hotel to meet my friends, I kept thinking about him. Ironically, we had talked for hours, and I did not even get his name. All I remember is that the conversation was so rich and fulfilling that I knew without a doubt I had to see him again. I had never felt such a physical and mental connection with a man before. I liked it, and I did not want to let it go. So why had I? I could have easily scheduled a time to see him again.

The next day, I returned to the café, hoping more than anything that he would be there. I knew it was a long shot. If we were supposed to meet, we would have said so the day before. It was my fault; I blew it.

As I neared the café, I could see the handsome man sitting at the same table we had occupied the day before. He was facing the water and drinking an espresso. My heart skipped a beat at the sight of him. As I walked up behind him, I said, "*Scuzi*, may I sit?"

He turned around with a big smile and gestured to the seat next to him as I had the day before.

"How long have you been here?" I asked.

"All day. I did not want to miss you in case you came in the morning, and when you didn't show, I knew you would come this afternoon. I knew you would come," he said, still smiling. "I think I've had too many espressos, though. I am quite jittery!"

I laughed, hoisted up my bag, and motioned for him to follow me. He stood up, laid a few euros on the table, and joined me on the sidewalk.

"Where are we going?" he asked.

"To get a better view," I said.

It was the perfect time of day, just like the day before, when I first met him. The sun was starting to dance on the water, making those sparkling reflections so bright before sunset.

We spent the entire summer together. It was truly a whirlwind romance. If you asked me today whether I would run off with a man I just met and get married, I would laugh in your face at the thought. I am practical and sensible. It did not fit my plan back then, but when you are young and in love, plans often go out the window. Besides, living life truly means living life. In my heart, I knew it was right. Who says you have to be engaged for so many months or years before you marry? When you are in love, nothing on Earth can rewrite what is already written.

My friends had begged me to come home with them, but they could tell I had made my decision, so they were beyond happy for me. We all had tried to follow the mantra "Go where life takes you," and this was where my life was taking me. No regrets.

Gino showed me up and down the Italian coast that summer, and I was the happiest I had ever been in my life. His outlook on life was ardent. We ate simply. We lived simply. We were high on the land and what it offered us. The feel of the water on our skin as we tiptoed into the sea, the unassuming splendor of the countryside as we picnicked in tiny villages, the rugged landscape as we drove through the mountains—these were enough to feed the mind. The sheer beauty of this painting coming to life was nourishing a long-neglected part of my soul. I was genuinely happy and in love. If I only could have bottled that feeling and kept it with me, taking sips to lift me when times would prove too hard to bear.

Gino proposed to me that September. I remember it clearly. We had spent a beautiful day together, swimming and sunbathing. We imagined our future together, and right then and there—my hair messy and full of salt, sand stuck to our bodies from dancing on the beach—Gino got down on one knee in front of me. I already knew I would spend the rest of my life with him, but seeing him kneeling before me was surreal. He did not have a ring, so he quickly fashioned one out of dried seaweed. Almost before I realized what he was doing, he uttered the most precious words: "Francesca, will you marry me?" While we probably could have married within the week, my only request was that I wanted our parents present. And so they were. We married the first week of October. The wedding was simple and sweet, just like our devotion to each other.

It was one of the best days of my life.

CHAPTER 3

AFTER MY FIRST ATTEMPT to start my day, I am back in the kitchen again. Nothing is different, yet I feel better. Perhaps I needed the extra sleep. I have a second chance to do something productive with my day.

I make my way over to the counter to make a pot of coffee. I know it sounds corny, but to me there is nothing better than a fresh cup of coffee in the morning. The first sip is like sunshine on my face: it instantly transports my mood. While I wait for the coffee to brew, I sit at the kitchen table. It is an old pine table we found at an estate sale years ago. I love old furniture; it is solidly built and more durable than most of the furniture sold today. It has a story to tell, and it slowly unravels its secret every time I sit. A deep scratch here or a burned spot there— not blemishes to make the table unwanted but character to add to its eclectic charm. I open my laptop, and before I know it, I fall into the internet abyss. Then I hear the ring of the landline over by the kitchen window.

I pick up the heavy, old-fashioned handset and say, "Hello?" We have an old phone. I seem to have a lot of old-fashioned pleasures. Our kitchen phone is so old that it has no display to show where the incoming call is coming from, and I like that. I love the excitement of wondering who could be on the other end and why they are calling me. Smartphones take that mystery away. And because I don't know who is calling, I must answer the phone politely. The simple phone etiquette that is increasingly falling by the wayside can change the course of a conversation.

"Hi, babe." It's Gino. "I have a minute before I meet with some clients."

Smiling at the thought of him wearing his work overalls and probably covered in wood shavings, I say, "Thank you for the beautiful flowers. I love them. I love you."

"I meant what I said, you know. You aren't alone. I know you have been having a hard time since you lost your job, and maybe for quite some time before that. We will figure this out. I have a great idea for tonight, but it's a surprise. I want you to get dressed up, and I will pick you up at seven."

"You aren't coming home first?"

"No, I have to work a little late. But trust me. You are going to love this. I love you," Gino says, and I hear the phone click.

I set the handset back in its cradle. I am curious to know what he has planned.

After fifteen years of marriage, he still always surprises me. There is never any assumption regarding our love for one another. I love how he looks at me and makes me feel, but most of all, I love that he loves me and lets me know it.

Since the bank closed, I have still tried to keep a routine. It helps me feel more productive. Even if nothing is pressing on my calendar for the day, I try to at least get outside for a walk with Luigi. The rain has finally begun to taper off to a drizzle, so I get up from the table and call out to Luigi. I walk down the hallway and find him curled up by the front door. He gingerly raises his head as if he is not sure whether he heard his name. Then his tail starts flapping against the floor, making a thumping sound, faster and faster, like a plane readying for take-off. I rub his head and say, "Come on, boy. Let's go for a walk." Convinced that he heard me, he jumps up and follows me as I make my way upstairs to get dressed.

I find a pair of yoga pants hiding underneath a pile of sweatshirts in my closet. Until the last few weeks, I have not needed them, and the ones I have worn are in the wash. I throw them on, along with a sweatshirt. I brush my teeth, grab a pony-tailer to pull back my unruly morning hair, and head back down the stairs, Luigi right behind me. He waits patiently while I put on my shoes and rain jacket. The jacket is teal, a color I love. It reminds me of a bright sky, and what better time to wear something so cheerful than in the rain? As I'm putting Luigi's harness and leash on him, I imagine what he would say if he were human. "Seriously, are you almost ready? This is taking forever." Finally, we head out the door.

A blast of cool, damp air hits my face, and I breathe in the scent of the rain and the leaves. It feels good to be outside. We go down the front walk and head toward the walking trails. I feel lucky to have such a nice trail system nearby. It is quiet and secluded; I consider it my sanctuary. The entire area where we live is quiet most of the time. I like it, but it gets lonely. It would be nice to live in town and have a few neighbors you could call to borrow a cup of sugar, if people even do that anymore, or share the day's news with. That's what I miss most about the bank. I realize now that it's not the job I miss but the chance to interact with people. I enjoyed going to work because it was like hanging out with family and friends all day. Being an extreme introvert, I find it hard to venture out of my world. The bank was where I connected with others. Now I have lost that, and I do not know how to find it again. That feeling of paralysis is what people do not understand. It is not that I do not want to help myself; it's that I can't. I am mentally and physically trapped, and I need some source of outside intervention to pull me out of my sinkhole and save me from drowning. Only people who have experienced this kind of anguish can understand the degree of suffering it causes.

Luigi and I head up the trail to the large open field. It is flanked by all kinds of big trees that provide welcome shade in the summer and a beautiful backdrop for a snow scene in winter. It is kind of like our town center but with nothing in it. The local kids use it as a campground when the weather is warm. It is like they are far away yet still under the watchful eyes of their parents. From a distance, you can hear them running around and see the flashlights flicker in the evening as they tell stories and toast marshmallows. It is comforting to hear the squeals of teens having fun and the sparkle of the lights that take on a magical glow in the darkness. It brings back wonderful childhood memories of playing flashlight tag and catching lightning bugs in the summer.

I head across the field and down to the creek bed. It is gushing now from all the rain we have had lately, but it looks pretty with all the trees. Pretty soon the water will turn to ice—that is if we get any cold weather this year. We live in Virginia—not quite northern Virginia, but more populated than other areas that used to be consistently cold, but the last few years have offered less and less winter. I circle the path that will eventually lead me back home. The path is so automatic that I stop thinking about the walk and become aware of the sinking pressure in my stomach. *I'm a smart, educated woman*, I think to myself. *Why am I just stuck?* Stuck in life, stuck in not finding a job, stuck in just everything. At some point my internal thoughts become verbalized, and suddenly I hear myself mumbling. "God, can't you hear me pleading for help? Some direction or inspiration or . . . anything?" Fortunately, no one is nearby to hear me ranting away. If I say it out loud maybe God will have a better chance of hearing me, or maybe it will give the universe a chance to respond. I am tired of this. I am tired of waking up every morning with this dreadful gloom hanging over me that I cannot escape and pretending to everyone in my orbit that I am fine. But why confide in them? They cannot change it. The gloom and the tears are a daily occurrence for me. It is almost as if I don't know what else to do. Maybe it is a form of absolution that helps me to momentarily reset.

When I look up again, Luigi and I are almost to the sidewalk in front of our house. I stand, staring up at it. Our house is nice, but it is not my dream house. It is a 1980s-style brick colonial. We bought it when we first married because it was what we could afford. Our thought was to live here a few years until we decided what we wanted to do and which direction to go. Once we moved in, though, we got used to the rhythm of life here. After a few years, the idea of moving fell off the radar. The only things I like about the house are the hardwood floors, kitchen, and tin roof. Everything else about it is so dated it looks like we live in an eighties sitcom. A bubble of laughter rolls out of me as I think about it. How had we never noticed these things? If we entertained frequently, we would have noticed, but we do not host many guests. We live far from any big cities, so our hosting is limited to holidays and the occasional visit from family.

Standing there, staring up at the house, I am unsure what to do next. I feel resentful about the mindset forming in my head. Luigi, bored with sniffing at the grass, pulls against the leash. Usually, I try to coax him in, but today it's the other way around. The rain picks up again, and we dash up the footpath to the front door and duck inside.

I take off Luigi's harness and leash and hang them on one of the hooks by the door. Luigi runs down the hallway before I have a chance to wipe his paws. I let him go.

"It's not like the floors don't need a good cleaning anyway," I say out loud. I peel off my rain jacket and hang it next to Luigi's leash to dry.

Rainy days always make me feel indolent. They are also good days to bake. As I start to form a plan for the next few hours, I feel a little reprieve from the thoughts running through my mind. I love the smell of cookies baking in the fall. It reminds me of coming home from school as a kid. My mom would be in the kitchen making cookies, and as soon as I came in from the cold, the warm, sweet smell would instantly make me feel safe and happy to be home. It is funny how vivid our childhood memories can be and how quickly they conjure up the feelings associated with them. To this day I love sweets of all kinds. Smiling, I walk into the kitchen, deciding to bake some chocolate chip cookies. I figure I have plenty of time to make a batch or two, even if I decide to go to yoga at two o'clock.

After spending the next hour and a half in the kitchen, I glance at the digital clock on the microwave. It is 1:12. I had better get going. It takes a good thirty minutes to get to the studio, assuming there are no traffic delays. While we do not have much traffic in this area, it seems that inevitably I get stuck behind a dump truck or a garbage truck on these winding two-lane roads. You never know what you will encounter, and I do not like to be late. Wrapping up the mess in the kitchen, I leave everything as it is until I get back. I turn off the oven and put some plastic wrap over the mixing bowl. I can deal with the mess when I get back. I call up to Luigi to say goodbye, then head out the door.

I started taking yoga classes years ago when I stumbled upon the studio while driving past it with a friend. She mentioned she had been taking classes and asked me to join her for a session. While I have always been active somehow, I embarrassingly had to admit that I did not know what yoga was, let alone what it could do for me. I jumped at the chance to learn something new. Of all the things I have tried over the years to vanquish thoughts of doom, yoga has been the most effective. It lets my thoughts melt away in a peaceful, fulfilling fashion. My favorite pose is at the end. After all the hard work of forming poses and breathing on cue, I am left lying on the mat in a state of total calm. By the end of class, I feel as if some magical transformation has been performed. I am a different person.

I arrive early and am settled and ready when class starts. "Inhale," says the instructor. "Exhale." Every syllable is stretched out like a rubber band. Over and over, I listen to the words and tell myself to breathe accordingly. I find that telling my mind to breathe can send a little recharge to my system.

"Inhale. Exhale." The words float around in my head like a song stretching out its chorus. Focusing on my breath, I will myself to let all my frustration seep out of me and into the universe. I let the wave of relief fill my body, replacing the frustration with a momentary feeling of hope. In this fleeting second, I feel power. I feel strong. I feel enabled. I feel promise—but, most important, I feel alive.

After class, I am lying on my mat, slightly dazed by the effort. I hear my friend Jane say, "Are we heading to the coffee shop?" On Tuesdays after class, a group of us always go to the coffee shop across the street.

"Yes, I would love that." Sometimes there are four or five of us, but today it's just Jane and me. Secretly, I am pleased.

Jane is my best friend. She works for a big publishing company, which offers her the chance to work from home, have a flexible schedule, and spend more time with her kids. She has beautiful long blond hair, a gorgeous smile, and an aura about her that makes people instantly comfortable. We have known each other since college. Living in different towns, we do not get to see each other often. It has been a few months since we last met up. Jane has been my best friend for so long that I can tell her anything and there is no judgment. She has her demons, and I have mine, yet we accept each other as we are. We talk about everything from politics to religion to family to life happiness and struggles. No topic is off-limits. That is what makes our conversations so exciting. Each of us propels the other, whether with a big new idea or the driving force to make it through the day.

Sometimes the coffee shop is so crowded there are no tables available. Today there are plenty. Jane and I order our usual—vanilla lattes and chocolate croissants—and chit-chat with George, the owner, while we wait for our order. George is in his late fifties and tall with a little pot belly and a long gray beard. His standard uniform is jeans and a flannel shirt, and that is when he is dressed up. He has a big, boisterous laugh, and his standard greeting to those he knows well is a big bear hug. He has owned this coffee shop for about ten years. He used to be a lawyer at a big financial firm, but then he decided to make a change and live his dream. So he bought this building, a former antique store in ruins, and restored it. The wood floors are original, and the high tin ceilings have never been painted. With the chandeliers, long curtains, and marble-topped bistro tables, it reminds me of a French café. Sometimes he has a live band on summer evenings. Music flows out the open doors and onto the sidewalk, drawing people in like moths to a flame. George does not look the part of a café proprietor, but that makes his place even more charming.

Jane and I grab our lattes and croissants and head to one of the tables by the window, eager to dig into the chocolate sweetness and sip from the cups brimming with frothy foam.

"Tell me what's new today," Jane says as she takes a sip of the latte.

"Do you really want to know?" I pause for a bite of the sweet dessert. "I feel like I haven't had anything new to add to the conversation lately. This morning was tough. Some days, I wake up and I am fine. I have the whole day to conquer and am excited at the possibilities. Other days, it is a struggle to get out of bed. I don't understand it. I have to plan things, knowing there is a possibility I can't follow through. I can do anything, yet I can't. I'm tired of this. Ever since the bank closed, I feel like

I have been spiraling. I feel trapped in my head, and whatever I try to do, I can't escape it."

"Does Gino know you've been feeling bad?" asks Jane as she cradles her warm cup.

"Yes, he knows. I thought I was doing a good job of keeping it to myself. I thought I could work through it. You know Gino's happy disposition; I didn't want to make him worry. But this morning he left me a gorgeous bouquet of roses and said I'm not alone and we'll get through this together. He is taking me out tonight. He wants me to get dressed up and says we can talk."

"Yep, you got lucky the day you met him. We were all secretly jealous but so happy for you," Jane says.

"He truly is a wonderful man."

"You know, Fran, sometimes we look so hard to find something. That seems to be the time when you can't find it . . . whatever it is. It seems to me that you need to stop internalizing everything. I know that's easier to say than do, but dwelling on what *is* won't help," Jane said as she took another sip of her latte.

"I know. You are one hundred percent right. I know this won't change overnight. I'm trying hard to take things moment by moment. Wasn't that our mantra in college? Live in the moment. No regrets. Just living happily. It is easy to slip away from the things that were always so important to us. I don't know what to do. All I know is that I can't continue living like this. I've got to do something."

Letting out a deep breath, I sit back in my chair and glance out the windows at the cars driving by. I can feel my frustration mounting. What I so easily dispelled in yoga class quickly filled my brain again. "Okay, enough is enough. I've had enough of the blues for today. Let's talk about you. I want to know what wonderful things are happening in your life."

"Charlie and I are celebrating our fourteenth anniversary tomorrow. I can't believe we've been together for nearly fifteen years," Jane says.

"That's right! What are you doing to celebrate?"

"Well, with four kids and all their activities, it would be too hard to get away, so we are celebrating as a family. We're having a formal pizza party. Everyone's going to dress up. The little kids are so excited," says Jane, laughing.

Giggling at the thought of a formal pizza party and smiling at the sweetness of their family time, I tell her: "You have a pretty great guy yourself."

We chat for another hour before we glance at our phones and see the time.

"Well, this has been great," I say. "I'm so glad you came to class today. I'm so glad *I* came to class today. I needed a friend today. I didn't realize how much."

As we stand up, grab our belongings, and make our way to the door, Jane says, "I'm always here for you. Sometimes talking out loud can help. You will find your way. It may seem daunting now, but you will. I have faith in you."

I smile and blink back a tear. We hug and say goodbye, then walk away.

Driving home from the coffee shop, I find myself smiling at the thought of Gino. I often wonder where my life would be now if we hadn't met all those years ago. It seems like it was only yesterday that we had the innocence of youth, knowing a lifetime of love was still ahead of us. Now here we are, fifteen years later. How quickly time has passed! I am so thankful that I followed my heart and gave my full trust to God that I was making the right decision. He knew best, and I had faith. If only all things worked out that way.

It is just after five in the afternoon when I get back to the house. Gino will be here at seven, and I want to be ready. It has been a while since we have gotten dressed up, and I want to look and feel my best for him. When I open the door, an overly thrilled Luigi greets me. He is always so excited to see me, no matter what. I love his happy presence. Do dogs ever feel sad? They always seem so jovial. If they get lonely spending their day in solitary confinement, they quickly forget about it. Luigi falls to the floor with his paws in the air. I laugh and give him a few belly rubs. "Come on, baby," I say. "Let's go outside." I open the door, and out he runs at lightning speed.

I head into the kitchen to clean it up. I turn on some music. I feel myself in a light-hearted mood. Thank goodness; I was worried I would not feel up to going out tonight, but I know that's the one thing I need. Besides, there is nothing I love more in this world than spending time with Gino. I start the playlist on my phone, and Van Morrison's "Days Like This" begins to play. Of all the songs next in the shuffle, I could not have picked a better one if I'd tried. I have my bad days and more than I want. While today's start may have been a little rocky, the finale will be worth it. I lived today. I struggled through my feelings and hurt. I cried. But I had a friend to confide in, and I will feel loved by my husband. Today, I lived, and that is worth the fight.

Luigi comes back inside, and I give him his dinner. Satisfied with the kitchen all cleaned up, I go upstairs. I chuckle at my thoughts from earlier in the day. We have a dated house. How could I have become so oblivious to it? Maybe that should be one of our topics for discussion tonight. What if we remodeled? Or moved? The thought of either excites me and, for a few moments, my sense of possibility is back.

I feel even better when I look at the clock and realize I have time for a long hot shower. After the dampness and chill of the day, the steam from the shower feels good. The sensation of the warm water flowing over my skin on a day like this is heaven. I plunge my face into the cascading waterfall, eager to wash away the day's grime. A passing thought reminds me of how bad I felt this morning, but I immediately shift my focus to what I will wear tonight. I think I will wear my black midi dress. I have not worn that dress in so long. It has three-quarter-length sleeves and a crisscross front with a black ribbon tie on the side. It is nothing special, but I love to wear it because it makes me feel pretty. I turn off the shower, grab a fresh towel from the shelf, and wrap myself up. Wiping off the mirror to see my reflection, I consider how much I have changed over the years. I recognize an older version of myself. Sometimes I feel older, and sometimes I feel younger. Right now, I feel just right.

Blow-drying my hair, the thought of Gino coming soon excites me. It's been a long time since we went out for a date night. It is the one thing I have been looking forward to all day. It's a chance to think about something new for the evening instead of analyzing every thought that enters my mind.

Walking into the bedroom, I slip into my dress and put on the finishing touches: my berry cream lipstick, diamond stud earrings, and a dab of Coco Chanel Eau de Parfum No 5. I grab my favorite black clutch with silver sparkles outlining the trim, slip into my black shoes, and make my way downstairs. I cannot help but feel that same excitement I felt the day I went back to see if Gino would be at the café. As the doorbell rings, my heart sings. As I come off the last step, I hear Luigi coming out of the kitchen, and I tell him to stay. I grab my black swing coat and open the door, and Gino is in a suit and tie, looking more handsome than ever. I fling myself forward and hug and kiss him as if I have not seen him in years.

CHAPTER 4

"WHAT A WELCOME! I should have done this sooner!" Gino stands back and looks into my blue eyes with his, mirroring mine. "You look absolutely stunning. But you always are to me in every way. I love you with all my heart." Softly his lips touch mine, and he gives me the lightest, most tender kiss with meaning more powerful than my heart can hold.

By the end of our kiss, I'm clinging to his shoulder for support. The emotion was enough to make my knees buckle. Italian men.

"Shall we go?" he says. It's a chilly evening, but the rain from earlier in the day has finally stopped. He locks the front door, then leads me toward the car with his hand on the small of my back, an act so intimate and modest it sends goosebumps down my back. He opens the passenger door, and I slide into the heated leather seat. He left the car running to keep it warm for me. I buckle myself in and burrow into the seat, ready for the evening ahead. Gino slides into the driver's seat and looks at me with a big smile.

I return his grin. "Where are we going?"

"I thought tonight we would recreate our first date. First stop, dinner at Marcelo's. It's not Italy, but it is as close as you could imagine."

Our first official date was in Italy, the night after I found Gino at the café. He asked me out for an evening of dinner and dancing and topped it off with a walk near the ocean and a bowl of gelato before he took me back to my hotel. How romantic it was for me. That was when I knew I wanted to spend the rest of my living days with Gino Martinelli.

"Marcelo's—is it in the old pharmacy building? I have wanted to try that place ever since they started advertising. They're open already? I thought they weren't going to open for another two weeks."

Gino says, "Hmm," and smiles.

When we pull into the parking lot, lights are on in the restaurant, but no other cars are around. I tell Gino I do not think they are open. The exterior of the restaurant is gorgeous. Miniature white lights are strung all around the entrance, and a beautiful, large wooden door with stained-glass windows beckons you to cross the threshold. Gino parks, gets out, walks around to the passenger side, and opens my door.

"What on Earth is going on?" I ask.

"Follow me." Gino leads me up the welcoming brick pathway to the entrance.

The door opens and a young man in a tuxedo says, "Welcome, Mr. and Mrs. Martinelli." He looks to be eighteen yet is comfortable in his uniform and well-practiced in his standard greeting routine. His dark hair and tan skin would make any young girl swoon. Grinning from ear to ear, I look at Gino as we follow the young man inside. The dining room is even more beautiful than the outside. The ceiling is open, showing off dark wood beams, and one wall is exposed brick. Flickering lights float magically around the room. As my eyes adjust, I see that each table has a glass globe candle holder with a candle suspended inside. The tablecloths are classic white. Alcoves offer more private seating. An Italian aura has been captured, both inside and out. I cannot imagine a more perfect setting for this special night.

The young man shows us to an already-set table and pulls out my chair. As we get settled, he fills our water glasses. "Mr. and Mrs. Martinelli, my grandfather said to tell you to have a wonderful time. The chef and I will bring out your food, and then you will be on your own. You can send a text to my grandfather when you leave, and he will lock up."

Gino says, "Thank you, Franco," and extends his hand. Franco accepts the gesture and looks pleasantly surprised at the unexpected kindness he feels being pressed into his palm. Franco bows and then disappears into the kitchen.

I smile wide at Gino. "This is amazing! How did you ever pull this off?"

"As it turns out, I met Mr. Marcelo Salvatore about six months ago. He loves carpentry and has been coming into the shop to have things made. We talked and developed quite a friendship over the last several months. He mentioned he was looking for a place to open an Italian restaurant. I told him about the old pharmacy, so he went to check it out. He thought it was perfect, and here we are." Gino picked up the wine carafe and filled our glasses. "I would like to propose a toast. To my beautiful wife and our life together. I can't imagine it any other way."

"Prost," we both say as we clink our glasses together. Tasting the sweet wine as it lingers on my tongue, I laugh. "Lambrusco! You even remembered the wine we drank all those years ago." Sitting back in our chairs, we share a smile and take each other in.

"There's more, too. He knows my father."

"You're kidding!"

"I know. Isn't it unbelievable? He was several years behind him in school, but his older brother was good friends with my dad. I mean, what are the chances? Of all places to open a restaurant, he picks a small Virginia town and meets a random person who has a connection to him from his birthplace."

"That's uncanny. I guess this is a small world."

As we engage in conversation, the chef and Franco bring out all the courses of the meal on a cart. They explain the entrees briefly and then depart, saying they don't want to intrude on our time. For the rest of the meal, Gino and I are alone, surrounded by this beautiful backdrop.

The food is sensational. Savoring bites, I close my eyes and am instantly transported to Portofino. So clearly, I can taste the Italian cuisine, smell the ocean water, hear the mingling of people with the music in the background, and feel the secluded world we left all those years ago. It is funny that in all these years, we have never been back. I guess we never thought about it.

As if listening to my thoughts, the song "Ti Amero" fills the air. It's the song we danced to on our first date. We were at an outdoor restaurant, and lights were everywhere, sparkling above us like brilliant stars dangling from the sky, so low that we could almost touch them with our fingertips. Gino asked me to dance. There was no dance floor, just the open space around the tables, most of which were occupied by other couples. We were the only ones dancing, but after a few moments, one by one, other couples rose from their tables and joined. It was one of the most beautiful, spontaneous scenes I have ever witnessed. I remember every detail of that evening: what I wore, how my hair was done, the feel of the beautiful summer night. But what I remember most was the feeling of floating on air as if I were living in a dream.

Gino pushes back his chair and walks around the table. Extending his right hand to me, he asks me to dance. From the moment Gino rang the doorbell this evening, I have felt as if I've stepped into a movie script. As we sway to the song now, my feelings are unlike anything I have experienced. It's different from the feelings of young love. It is the feelings of fifteen years of marriage wrapped up into this one intimate moment. Movement to movement, breath to breath, Gino twirls me around the room. Wrapped in his arms, I know there is no place on Earth I would rather be than living my life in tandem with this man.

We enjoy the rest of our meal. Dessert is amazing. There's even hot coffee in an insulated carafe. When we're done, Gino texts Marcelo. Before long, we see a pair of headlights through the window and hear activity in the kitchen. Gino helps me into my coat, then picks up his coat and escorts me back to our car. I slide into the passenger seat in a blissful state. Maybe it is the wine, maybe it is the satiated feeling from all the wonderful food, maybe it's the memories or the evening itself, but whatever this feeling is, I don't want the evening to end.

Gino drives us home. He parks in the driveway, which is odd. He gets out of the car again and walks around to open my door. As he helps me out of the car, he says, "I know it's getting late, but there is one more stop we need to make." He leads me away from the house, and we walk arm in arm up the trail to the large open field. The full moon illuminates our path as if a spotlight were trained on us. As we approach the last of the trees before the open field, I notice a cooler and a blanket.

"Someone must have forgotten their cooler," I say, glancing up at Gino.

"I believe that is for us," Gino replies. "We couldn't let our second first date end without some gelato. Remember how we searched all over that night, looking for a place that was still open, and then after we found it, we walked down by the water? We don't have a beach, but we have a creek and some store-bought gelato. That will have to do."

"That will definitely do," I say, reaching out as Gino hands me a small carton. We wrap the blanket around our shoulders and eat our gelato. When we're done, we gaze at the stars. Just as I think the moment cannot get any better, he kisses me and tells me how much he loves me. The man of my dreams is standing next to me. I could not have envisioned a better evening. For the last several hours I have been transported to another dimension, leaving behind my struggles and embracing my present.

It's late now and getting cold, so we walk back to the house shivering, arm in arm. It has been a long day for both of us.

Lying in bed, my husband sleeping peacefully next to me, I slowly review the night's events in my head. I'm still giddy from the surprise of it all. Knowing the sheer effort he put into planning the evening for me makes my heart melt. For the first time in a while—not wanting to fall asleep yet, but knowing I am fading fast into the abyss—I thank God for giving me this evening.

CHAPTER 5

I hear Gino coming out of the bathroom and can tell by his shadow that he is fully dressed. It was still dark out. I roll over to see the time. It's just shy of five in the morning. I raise my head and sleepily ask, "Why are you getting up so early today? Come back to bed."

"Go back to sleep, babe. I have a client at seven and want to have my designs and everything out ahead of time." Leaning over, he gives me a kiss on the forehead and says he will see me tonight. "I love you."

"I love you, too." I lay my head on the pillow and drift off to sleep.

I love Gino's dedication to his art, craft, and business. I do not have the discipline to get up so early. I like my sleep. He has always been that way, though, from the beginning. He is laid back and goes with the flow, but when it comes to his work, he seeks perfection. That is why his business has done so well over the years. When Gino was young, his grandfather told him stories of his great-grandfather and the beautifully handcrafted fishing boats he built. They were so good that people came from all over Italy—most of Europe, really—to buy them. He loved the craft, and it showed. The business was passed down to Gino's grandfather, but when it was Gino's father's turn, he wanted nothing to do with boatbuilding. He had desires to travel and move to the United States. He did not want to be tied down when there was an entire world to see. So Gino's grandfather eventually sold the business, but not before he taught his grandson a few of the old ways. Gino never forgot, and he has a knack for woodworking. He knew wherever he ended up, that is what he was meant to do.

When I met Gino in Italy, he had been there for about a year and a half. He had done a little family research and inquired about starting his business. Even though the business would be stateside, he wanted true Italian craftsmanship, so he went back to where it all started, his grandfather's store. The connections and contacts he made during that trip have been invaluable. The authenticity of his work is what shows, and that is what sells. He has worked so hard over the years and he has made a name for himself under the banner of authentic Italian wood crafts by Gino Martinelli. The demand for boats is not high in the area we live, however, so his attention has primarily been on household furniture. He has wonderful clients and a lot of repeat customers, but I know that, deep down, he wants to build boats. Thinking about that, I start to wonder why we live here. Why not somewhere closer to the water? Is it time for a change? Maybe that's what Gino and I both need.

I'm awakened by Luigi sniffing my side of the bed. He does not bark, but he's smart and starts to move around so you know it's time to get up. "Okay, baby. I'm getting up." But I lie there, stealing a few more moments under the warmth of the covers. I am instantly transported by my feelings to the night before. The sun is shining this morning; I can see the brightness coming in around the sides of the shades. How much easier it is to get up when it is sunny out. I feel like my disposition often reflects the weather. With a mood ready to welcome the coming day, I get out of bed and begin my morning routine. First stop, belly rub and kisses for Luigi, followed by his morning jaunt outside.

Later, I start a pot of coffee. Leaning against the kitchen counter, I notice how good I feel this morning. Only yesterday, I'd felt as if the world were caving in. Then again, most of the last few months have felt that way. The phone rings, and I pick up quickly. "Hello?" I sing.

"Hey, babe," Gino says.

"Good morning! How did your meeting go?"

"It was better than I expected. I have a new customer. His wife wanted a twelve-seat table for their new house, so I had some ideas to show them. They loved them, but not only that, the husband said he wanted me to build him a fishing boat. It's been a long time since I've had that request! Anyway, I was calling to tell you I had a great time last night. We need to get out more often, you and I. I know I spend long days with the business and being an hour away doesn't make it easier."

"I had a wonderful time last night, too. I can't tell you how much better I feel this morning. Thank you for all you did for me. And I know how much you love your work. I want you to know how proud I am of you. I'm sorry I haven't told you that lately, but I think it all the time."

"Babe, you don't have to thank me for anything, and I know how you feel. You show me every day. Listen, I have to go. I should be home around seven tonight. Pizza and a movie?"

"That sounds great. See you tonight."

The coffee maker beeps as I hang up the phone. I pour a cup of coffee and wonder what's next. Suddenly I feel the sinking sensation starting to return. Why? Why do I feel so useless? Ten minutes ago, I was happy and fine, and now I can feel the gloom crowding my space, looming over me, waiting for some small opening to enter my mind. I call my friend Jane in hopes that the feeling will recede, but there is no answer. I hang up without leaving a message.

I sit at the table with my cup of coffee and turn on my computer. I start looking for jobs. I have got to find something. I can be anything, do anything—but what? My frustration mounts. I can feel my heart racing, and my eyes well up to the point that I can barely see the computer screen. What am I good at? I have been searching for that answer my entire life. What makes me happy? Am I living my life all wrong? Is my focus too self-centered? Am I the only one who gets these damned thoughts—the only one who gets disheartened to such an extreme?

"God," I say aloud, "please listen to me. I have faith. I believe. I pray. I just need some direction. I know I ask and think it every day, but why am I alive? What is my purpose here? I can't keep living like this." I feel as if I am living on borrowed time. One day the end will come, and I will still question my purpose. There have been moments in my life worth living, but there have also been so many moments where I just exist. I am tired of existing. I want to live.

Tired of my depressing thoughts, I decide to take Luigi out for a walk. I get dressed, then call to Luigi, who is sleeping by the front door. His head pops up the moment he hears his name. His eagerness makes me laugh. Outside, it's cool and the sunshine feels good on my face. I decide to walk fast, let the sunshine recharge me, and refocus my mood. I am going to find a way to make this day count.

After our walk, as soon as we get inside, Luigi runs down the hall. The bright sun streaming in the door reveals how dirty the floor is. Luigi's fur seems to fly everywhere; with the amount that builds up, you would think we have a white carpet instead of wood floors. Maybe I'll start the day with a good cleaning. A clean house always gives me the good feeling of having accomplished something. First, though, I want to drink my coffee. The old cup is still sitting on the counter. I dump the contents down the drain, then pour a fresh cup. I sit at the computer for a few minutes, staring at the screen, and randomly start clicking on old files. Some of them are so old I had forgotten all about them. One is titled "Diary, June, Portofino"—it's the journal I kept that summer after college. I open it and start reading. After reading the first entry, I cannot stop. I keep reading until halfway through that summer trip. I kept this journal because I wanted to remember everything: all the experiences, food, people, and culture, but mostly the memories.

I'm so caught up in reading that I almost don't hear the house phone ring.

I answer and hear Jane's voice on the other end. "Good morning."

"Good morning," I reply. "How did your anniversary pizza party go?"

Jane laughs and says, "It was great. We all dressed up. The kids conked out early, so we opened a bottle of wine and spent the evening just the two of us. It was perfect. How was your evening with Gino?"

"Amazing. I could not believe what he did for me. He took me to Marcelo's. Dinner, dancing, and gelato. He recreated our first date!"

"Wow, that's wonderful. Hey, I thought Marcelo's wasn't open yet?"

"It's not. The owner is one of Gino's new clients, and I guess they became fast friends. So we got to eat there all by ourselves. It was the first time in a long time that I enjoyed being in the moment, you know? And we talked a lot. It was nice to be together and not worry about anything else."

"I'm glad you had a great time. Sometimes an evening out puts a new twist on everything. You know, see things from a different perspective."

"You're right. It did help, at least for the night. Hey, you'll never guess what I just found. My old journal I kept on our trip that summer after college. I was just reading through it when you called. I forgot so many of the adventures we had that summer."

"That was an amazing trip. One of the best times of my life."

"Mine, too," I say.

"I'm sorry to cut this short," Jane says, "but I have to run. Ballet practice."

"Sure, thanks for calling. Talk soon," I say, and we hang up.

My spirits are lifted from the phone call. I close the computer. It's already past one in the afternoon, and I've procrastinated long enough; it's time to tackle the floors. Luigi's blond hair is everywhere. I love him so much, though. Hairy floors are part of the package. I turn on some music, and "Dreams" by The Cranberries begins to play. It is my favorite song. I am dancing around as I clean. My floor cleaning turns into a whole-house cleaning spree. I'm so engrossed in getting everything done that I ignore the constant rumbling in my stomach. I hadn't wanted to spoil my appetite for pizza later by eating a big lunch, so I had figured I would get a snack and then keep on cleaning. But I never even stopped for the snack. I guess I hadn't realized how much cleaning I had to do, and I must not have noticed that the light outside was slowly fading. The next time I looked outside, it was dark. I let Luigi out for a few minutes. By the time we come back in, I'm shivering. I feed Luigi, put the cleaning supplies away, then head up the stairs and jump in the shower.

Gino gets home as I'm getting out. "Hey babe," I hear him yell up the stairs.

"I'll be right down. I just got out of the shower," I yell. I throw on a pair of comfy jeans and my favorite pink cashmere sweater, slide my feet into my warm slippers, and head down the stairs. My hair is still damp from the shower and giving me a chill. Maybe we can build a fire tonight. I love the smell of a wood-burning fireplace. I walk into the kitchen and find Gino standing, unable to move because Luigi is sitting on his feet and begging for attention. Laughing at the sight, I walk over and give Gino a kiss. "I'm starving," I say. "Are you hungry? Want to order from Napoli?"

"Yeah, that sounds good. Let's get pepperoni and green pepper. Do you want anything else on it?"

"Mushrooms, too," I say.

Gino finishes giving Luigi undivided attention and then picks up the phone to place the order. While he's doing that, I throw a salad together and pull out two wine glasses from the kitchen cabinet.

"It should be here in half an hour," Gino says as he grabs a bottle of red wine from the rack and begins to open the bottle. Pouring us each a glass, he hands me one and begins to tell me about his day.

As he recaps what he had told me on the phone earlier this morning, I cannot help but notice how enthusiastic and alive he is now. Gino is always happy, but tonight, he is *alive*. It is because he is going to build a boat. Why am I just noticing this now? I feel as if lately I have become acutely aware of things I never paid much attention to. Have I not been paying attention all these years? Have I been hearing only what I want to hear? As Gino talks, I listen. I really listen. After describing his day, he leans against me, embraces me with his arms, and kisses me on the cheek.

"I'm going to go build you a fire," he says.

At the sound of the doorbell, I grab the salad bowl, wine, and plates and head into the living room. Soon Gino walks in with the pizza. It smells so delicious, and I realize again how hungry I am. Pizza and a movie by the fireplace is my idea of a perfect late-October evening. I know Gino and I are together every evening, but each night is different, and I never want to miss it. I cherish our nights curled up, entwined in each other's arms. I have been spoiled having him all to myself all this time, and I never want it to stop.

CHAPTER 6

THE HOLIDAYS—WITH ALL the traditions handed down, created, and added to—are my favorite time of year. This year, despite my best efforts, nagging feelings of self-doubt threaten to overshadow my holiday spirit. Since I was laid off from my job, the months have flown by. Ironically, each day seems longer than the last.

Each day, I yearn for the evening so I can get some reprieve from my thoughts. Where is the time going? Why have I not found another job? How can I face another day? I am angry with myself for being an educated woman who cannot find her place. No matter how hard I try, the hole I'm in gets deeper. My mind holds me back; I try to escape it, but I get sucked back into this fog. The world is changing around me, and I am having an arduous time keeping steps. It is too advanced, too fast, too self-centered. I have somehow gotten lost in this constant spiral of time, and instead of getting off and participating, I spin faster and faster. I try to stay busy and be productive, but I cannot help wondering how others see me. Do they think I'm lazy? Lacking ambition? No goals or dreams? Maybe that's how I see myself. The reality is that I am none of those things. I am not lazy, especially regarding the things I love. I do not lack ambition. When I have something I want, I am ambitious. I have goals and dreams. The challenge is making those goals and dreams a reality. I have a problem I cannot solve myself, and no amount of thinking and dwelling on it will change it. I need to figure out how to disconnect myself from my thoughts and connect myself to the world.

I keep questioning my daily existence. I feel like I need more than a hobby or projects around the house. I need to be doing something that fulfills me. But it is difficult to look for something when you have no clue what you're looking for.

A few years ago I inquired about volunteering at my church. When I made it clear that I did not have kids, they suggested devoting my time to prayer. That response dumbfounded me. It changed my view of our church but made my private devotion to God stronger. I looked at other local charities, but nothing panned out. I called to follow up, and they said they were still processing background checks and references. It was almost harder than trying to find a job. I had all this time to give and nowhere to give it. To be honest, I could have tried harder, but the experience made me feel invisible. I believe in the proverb by Paul Coelho, "When you want something, all the universe conspires in helping you to achieve it." Sometimes it feels as if the universe can't hear me.

I find it ironic that a world so full of people can sometimes be such a lonely place. It is the feeling of being at a party where you don't know anyone. I would rather be alone in my house than invisible to a house full of strangers.

While my feelings are at the forefront of my thoughts, I consciously try to stay optimistic and not think about my circumstance until the New Year. It would be selfish of me not to be joyous and thankful for what I have. I resolve to embrace this festive time rather than allow my haunting thoughts to ruin it.

Halloween has already come and gone, and we are looking toward Thanksgiving. Suddenly the days seem to be moving faster. I cannot tell if it's because I am getting older or because each day is a repeat of the day before. I am consumed with planning and preparations to host Thanksgiving dinner.

I am looking forward to a busy house: the sound of family and friends talking and catching up, festive holiday décor strewn about the house, kids running around, and most of all, the smell of pies baking in the oven.

Growing up it was always the three of us—my parents and me. I have a close relationship with them even though we cannot see each other often. They are coming here for Thanksgiving, and Gino's parents are coming from New Jersey. In past years Gino and I have traveled to spend Thanksgiving with one set of parents or the other, but this year we will all be together, which is rare.

Aside from our parents, Jane and her family are coming, as are some friends of Gino and several people I know from the bank. I had not kept in touch with my former co-workers since we lost our jobs, and I invited them, thinking maybe some of them could use a friend as much as I could. I am glad I extended the invitation. My friend Kathleen's husband passed away a month after the bank closed. She has no other immediate family, so she was excited about the invitation. I wish I had reached out to her sooner.

With the guest list up to twenty-seven, we are planning for quite a celebration, and the preparations are enough to thrust me into all-out party mode. For a few weeks I'm so busy that I have no time to think of my chronic pleas to God for help.

A week before Thanksgiving, when all my planning is done and only some finishing touches remain, I start to relax from my busy mode. Sitting in the kitchen one evening with the computer open, I see the old files of my journal staring back at me. I have not looked at them since before Halloween. I must have over sixty entries. Indulging myself, and always eager for respite from my thoughts, I start reading again. Some of the notes and comments I wrote make me laugh. Before long, I am fully engrossed by the words on the screen. As if some force propels me, I start taking the notes and rewriting them into actual sentences. Before I know it, I have two paragraphs written and then a page. I'm not sure where the words are coming from, but they flow from my typing fingers like musical notes from an instrument.

I sleep well that night and wake up around dawn. Standing in front of the kitchen window with a blanket draped over my shoulders, I watch the sun rise. An orange glow begins to shimmer on the horizon, and with every passing moment, it gets bigger and bigger. The sky is a beautiful panorama of brilliant pinks and baby blues. Taking a deep breath, I say a silent prayer. I pray I will have the strength to fight for what I am looking for, and I pray for all the people like me struggling to find their paths. The sight of this incredible sunrise is enough to shock my system and remind me that life is not about taking but giving and appreciating the simple natural beauty that life offers. Coffee in hand, I walk over to the table. I sit, open the computer, and begin to fill the empty pages.

CHAPTER 7

I step outside with an umbrella to greet our guests as they begin arriving on Thanksgiving Day. A drizzle started a few moments ago, but instead of dampening the mood, it only makes the house cheerier and more welcoming. A steady stream of people comes in the front door. Coats and umbrellas line the front hall. Gino is inside acting as bartender. When all the guests are inside, I turn and look at the house. Through the windows I can see glowing light and people eating and drinking, talking and listening, laughing and hugging. The house is so full of life and excitement that it looks like a Thomas Kinkade painting. I breathe in the cool autumn air and think the smell of chimney smoke only adds to the loveliness of a beautiful holiday celebration. It is one of those rare moments when you catch a glimpse of other people's happiness from the outside and know you are not just admiring the scene but can be one of the lucky few to partake in the joyous occasion inside. My heart is happy. I step inside, knowing all is right in my world.

Jane gives me a hug. "Fran, the house looks beautiful. I love what you did with the decorations. And the appetizers are to die for!"

"Wait until you try the desserts," I say, smiling. "I'm so glad you, Charlie, and the kids could spend the holiday with us. It's nice to see the house full of people. It hasn't looked this way in so long."

"I'm glad we didn't have to travel this year. Charlie's family is all over the place, and you know my parents went on a cruise. It's so nice to spend the day with you and Gino. The kids are thrilled to be here, too. Gino spoils them rotten. This might have to be a new tradition."

As we walk arm and arm to the kitchen, Jane whispers to me, "I'm so excited, I can't hide it anymore—I'm pregnant! Don't say anything; I haven't told Charlie the news yet."

"Oh Jane, that is such wonderful news! When are you planning to tell him?"

"Tonight, I think. I know he will be happy, but I'm still nervous."

As if he knows we are talking about him, Charlie walks into the kitchen. "Hey, ladies, Gino sent me in here for more ice, and he said we're running low on some of the appetizers."

Charlie is an English professor. His brown hair is graying slightly at the temples, and he wears his glasses perched on his nose in a way that makes him look distinguished. Yet his large frame and athletic posture hint at his original dream: he once played as a quarterback for Boston College and had a real prospect of turning pro. Unfortunately, an accident left him with a permanent injury to his leg, so he earned a doctorate instead. He has been a professor for the last fifteen years. His success comes from relating so well to his students.

I grab a bag of ice from the freezer and hand it to Charlie, and he looks at me and back at Jane. Casting a look at each other, Jane and I smile. "What's going on? Anything I need to know about?"

"No, honey," Jane says, escorting him to the kitchen door. "We'll get the food and be right out." As soon as he leaves, we both burst out laughing.

"Jane, I haven't felt like this in a while. I'm just so full of joy I can't contain it. I'm so happy you guys are here, and to top it off, your great news!" We grab the vegetable plates and canapés and head into the living room. The thought of being so happy with my friends and family surrounding me is a feeling I do not want to let go. I want the evening to last as long as it possibly can.

Gino is in the corner fixing drinks with an apron tied around his waist. Laughter I cannot contain bubbles up as I head over to him. I love how he plays his part. He is an entertainer, for sure. Everyone around him listens intently as if he is the only person in this room of twenty people. He has a gift for commanding attention simply by sharing his enthusiasm and spirit. I love seeing him in his element and happy. I think we need to update this house if we plan to stay.

I stand next to Gino and kiss him on the cheek. Gino turns toward me and plants a big one on my lips, and whistles and cheers ring out. So caught off guard, I blush before regaining my balance. I love this man.

"Does everyone have a glass?" Gino yells out.

"We need a couple of glasses over here," someone answers. As Gino pours a few more glasses of champagne and passes them over, he turns to me and, with a wink, hands me a glass of pink champagne, knowing it is my favorite. He thinks of everything and always knows how to put on the finishing touches. Now Gino hops onto a chair and calls everyone to gather around.

"First of all, Fran and I would like to thank all of you for coming today to spend Thanksgiving with us." Gesturing with open arms, he says, "There is no better time of year to tell the people who hold special meaning for us just how thankful we are to have you in our lives. We all have challenges, and we may try to conquer them ourselves, but it's important to remember that we have each other to lean on for support." He looks at me with softness in his eyes before continuing. "We are grateful to all of you for sharing this day with us, and we wish you a happy Thanksgiving. To family and friends!"

"To family and friends!" everyone echoes back, holding their glasses high. I look around at so many good people standing together and my eyes well up.

"I would also like to propose a toast to my wife of fifteen years, Fran. We've been together a long time, baby, and I'm looking forward to spending the next fifteen beside you. Thank you for planning this night and making it special for all of us. To Fran!" Gino says, raising his glass.

In unison, the crowd echoes back, "To Fran!"

The toasts go on for the next twenty minutes. The more toasts we take, the more our glasses need filling, and with all the eating and drinking, the party is brought to life.

The evening is a complete hit. It's nearly one in the morning before we say goodbye to the last of our guests. Our parents, exhausted from their travels and the grandeur of the party, retire to their rooms. Gino and I go about the house turning off the lights and locking doors, with Luigi following us. I am still giddy with excitement. The holiday season is upon us. We had a great party—even better than I anticipated. And Gino will be off for the next week. I am perfectly happy right now.

As we head upstairs together, Gino tells me once more that the party was wonderful. "I loved seeing you so happy, Fran. Oh, and Charlie said you and Jane were all hush-hush about something. What was it?"

Looking into Gino's face, I smile and give him a kiss. "You'll find out soon enough."

The long-awaited moment of falling into bed is pure heaven. My mind is blank, my tummy is full, and I lay my head on the pillow and savor the feeling of sleep taking me away.

The week following Thanksgiving is full of holiday-making memories. We take our parents to Christmas shows and concerts and do lots of Christmas shopping. We take down all the Thanksgiving décor and spend several days putting up the Christmas decorations. On the last day of our parents' visit, we go to a cut-your-own Christmas tree farm. A carriage ride takes us to the site, and the men take turns sawing while our mothers and I sip hot chocolate. It's a wonderful bonding time that has been long overdue. Such opportunities do not often present themselves. I have learned recently, however, to take advantage of the time we are given and make things happen when I can. I make a mental note not to let so much time pass before we do it again. Family is important to me, and not seeing each other often is heartache.

Saying our tearful goodbyes the following day, we vow to get together again by summer's end. I plan to hold everyone to it.

CHAPTER 8

THE DAYS BETWEEN THANKSGIVING and New Year's always seem magical to me. The stores are beautifully decorated, people are happy and even take to saying kind words to strangers, the air is fresh, the Christmas lights dazzle everywhere you turn your head, and most of all, if we are lucky, the ground will have its first covering of snow. The days have that simple, lighthearted feel that all is right with the world.

It is already the second week of December. Gino is putting in a few days at work this week, so he has already left for the shop while I wake up. It is the first time I have been alone since before Thanksgiving. I have always needed solitude; it's a form of retreat that restores the energy that being social drains from me, allowing me to be more amicable when I am in the presence of others. And being alone is one of the things I am most afraid of. It is a conundrum. To maintain equilibrium, I must find the perfect balance. Today, the silence is overwhelming. After days of guests, activities, and conversations, I feel as if a loud television has suddenly been placed on mute. My childhood home was always full of friends, family, and neighbors. The constant chaos of people coming and going was comforting. There was something soothing in knowing I was always surrounded by the people I loved the most. I never dreamed I would one day live in an empty house.

Luigi needs to go out, so I kick the covers back and get out of bed. I wrap myself in my robe to push away the morning chill. While having a full house at Thanksgiving was comforting and I loved every minute of it, I am looking forward to heading downstairs, turning on the Christmas lights, and drinking my first cup of coffee in solitude.

I know the feeling will begin to dissipate sooner than I think. I am slowly beginning to understand that needing solitude does not mean I never need people. People need companionship. We were not meant to live on this earth alone. I have always been an introvert and being around people at the bank was more important to me than I realized. Perhaps these last several months have been doing more for me than I realize. Maybe it allows me to reflect on my past to help me decide my future.

Luigi follows me down the stairs. As I walk into the kitchen, the phone rings. I wonder who would be calling this early.

"Hey, good morning! I didn't wake you, did I?" Jane asks.

"No, I've been up. I'm just making some coffee. I can't believe we haven't talked since the party."

"I know. I knew you had company, and we ended up having some. Charlie's brother and his family stopped by for a few days. So, I wanted to tell you . . . I told Charlie! He's so thrilled about the news." I could tell from the sound of Jane's voice that she was grinning from ear to ear.

"Can I tell Gino? He asked me that night after the party what we were chatting about, but I didn't say anything."

"Absolutely! I can already hear Charlie and Gino talking like it's going to be a boy," she laughs.

We spend the next forty-five minutes talking about our plans for the upcoming holidays and making time to get together. When I get off the phone, I realize I never started the coffee. I feel like I cannot function without it, so I do that before anything else.

While the coffee is brewing, I head upstairs to get dressed and straighten up. I put on a touch of makeup and comb my hair. As soon as I hear the gurgle of the coffee maker, I smile and head back to the kitchen. I pour my coffee, then get out the cream and sugar. I like my coffee sweet with lots of cream and sugar. I pause for a moment and consider using less sugar today or even cutting it out altogether, but that thought lasts a mere second. I like coffee, and if I am going to drink it, I am going to enjoy it. And with that, I take that first sip of the day.

I sit at the kitchen table, open my computer, and scroll down to the file I saved as "Journal Rewrite." I read what I have written so far, then write more. It feels effortless. Ironically, I never liked writing in college. I would stare blankly at the keyboard for hours, willing the words to come but unable to find them. But now I am surprised at how easily the ideas develop in my head. As I read the notes I wrote all those years ago and think back to the memories I have filed away in my mind, the pages come to life. The more I type, the more excited I get. When I finally look at the clock, I am stunned to see that it's twelve-thirty. "Well, I'm glad I got dressed," I say out loud.

I need a break and want to get out of the house even though I have no errands to run. I let Luigi out for a few minutes while I grab my keys and my light-blue satchel and put on my belted brown coat. The temperature has dropped a lot over the last several days, so I grab my matching blush-colored hat and mittens. I love the feeling of mittens; it's like wrapping my hands in a blanket, and mittens always keep my hands warmer than gloves. With no specific destination in mind, I set out on the road.

It feels good to drive. My mind has been so consumed with planning for the holidays, cleaning the house, and hosting family that I have not had much time to let my mind run free and decompress. I suppose in some way that is for the better. The more I think about the future and my lack of direction, the more I get depressed, and that is a path I would do anything to avoid. But now, I realize all the prepping and hosting I have been doing lately is what has kept me happy. I love staying busy and having a purpose. My time has been occupied with things to keep me from stressing about the future and losing myself in my mind.

With all the thoughts processing around in my head, I forget how long I've been driving. Only when I see the exit that leads to Gino's shop do I realize I've been on the highway for over an hour. I take the exit and turn onto Main Street. I think back to the last time I was here and am ashamed to realize it was over three years ago. Obviously when I was working it would have been difficult to leave work and drive an hour each way to visit the shop. But I've been out of work since the summer. Why didn't I come out sooner? Gino never said anything about it, and it never occurred to me that he might like some company.

I park on Main Street near the shop entrance. The building looks beautiful. When we bought the old brown barn, it was practically uninhabitable, an eyesore that the town had slated for demolition. But Gino has great vision. We bought it, and with a lot of hard work, Gino restored the original structure and turned it into one of the more attractive shops on Main Street. It's painted creamy white with dark brown trim and has a balcony across the second floor deep enough for a person to stand on, yet it still has a rustic look perfect for a store with a working woodshop. Gino has his winter decorations outside: a portable potbelly stove, a bench with blankets for passersby, and white lights strung around the doorway.

As I go inside, the old bell above the door rings. As I look around, I can understand why it is so hard for people to pass without wanting to buy something. The place takes my breath away. White lights hang from the rafters. Lovely wood carvings parade around the spacious shop, ringed with furniture displays. And, if that is not enough, at the center of the space is the workshop where Gino performs his craft. The smell of freshly cut wood as I breathe in deep makes me feel like I am in a forest. It is as authentic as you can get—it is like walking back in time to an old-world Italian shop. When people see that it is all handmade, they want to buy. Gino's shop is not just a store; it's a destination—almost another world.

Gino's work is nothing short of miraculous. He inherited his gift for the craft. As I look around, though, I realize how much of this shop is everything but the beautiful, handcrafted fishing boats Gino has always dreamed of building. With such a gift, it is a shame that he's not building boats. He has made a name for himself with furniture, though; for that, he should be proud. He has a following and pulls customers from all around the region. Still, if we lived near the water, he could focus on building those beautiful boats.

Hearing the bell jingle, Gino comes walking around the corner. "Fran!" he belts out. He picks me up and swings me around in a circle while giving me a kiss.

"Oh, Gino! I'm so glad I stopped in."

"This is such a pleasant surprise. What brought you out here? Is everything okay?"

"Yes, yes. I was working on some things this morning and needed to get out of the house. I'm sorry I didn't call first, but I was out for a drive. You've been on my mind a lot lately, and then I realized how close I was. Maybe my mind was trying to tell me something."

"Well, I am so happy to see you."

"This place is amazing. I'm so ashamed of myself, Gino. I can't believe how long it's been since I've been up here."

"Fran, you have enough things on your mind—and it's a long drive. You have absolutely no reason to be sorry," Gino says as he wraps me up in his arms.

A feeling of shame still haunts me, though, and I soon push away.

"Even so—I can't believe it never occurred to me to come out this summer. You mentioned you could use some help. I could be that help, and I didn't even pay attention to that." Tears start to creep down my cheek. I am not sure why. I think it is pure guilt that I never showed much interest in Gino's work all these years. It's as if I have taken for granted all that he does. "I've been so consumed with myself lately." Shocked by my revelation, I cannot hold back the tears, and they begin to pour out of me like the river over Niagara Falls. Fortunately, there are no customers in the store now.

"Fran, honey, there's nothing to be upset about. You have your life to lead. You have been under a lot of stress these last several months," Gino says as he hugs me and kisses me on my forehead.

"I know," I say, "but it's no excuse. I love this store, and I look around and see the beauty of it. You have poured your heart into it. Anyone can see that. I could have helped you all these years, but I never even asked. You tell me things, so I don't think to ask, but it's so selfish of me. I have been so hurtful to you, Gino. I'm so sorry. I'm so sorry." I'm crying even harder. Gino, as magnificent of a man as he is, holds me tightly in his arms with an embrace so loving that I can feel his heartbeat in sync with mine.

After several minutes of pouring out my tears, I can finally pull myself together. I am not sure where the over-emotional feelings came from, but I feel like they've been building up for some time, waiting for something to trigger the catastrophic release. Surprisingly, through the flushing of my tears, the warmth of Gino's embrace, and the calming beauty of this shop, I feel good. I feel as if I was led here for this single purpose. Perhaps I have unresolved feelings pent up over years of neglecting what's important to me—not by conscious choice but because of sheer ignorance and circumstance. Maybe this is an eye-opener for me, a reminder of what is most important in my life and that, while I cannot change my past actions, I can make changes for a better future.

Coming to my senses, I take the tissue Gino hands me, wipe my tears away, and blow my nose. Gino grabs my hand and shows me around the shop, and as we pass a mirrored hutch, I notice my eyes are red and swollen. Gino is excited to show me the table he is working on and the designs he has drawn for pieces he wants to make. Then I hear the ring of the bell over the door. Two customers come inside, talking, then stop and gasp at the beautiful creations displayed before them. I hear them taking deep breaths as they marvel at the uniqueness and grandeur of the place. Shortly the bell rings again, and again, and again. Giving me a kiss and a wink, Gino sets off to greet the visitors.

Taking care to hide my appearance from the customers, I walk around the store again to admire Gino's beautiful creations. They're inspiring. I feel better knowing Gino and I are in a good place and realizing some things in my life need to change. I overhear two customers talking. "This looks likes Santa's workshop!" . . . "What a brilliant idea." . . . "Look at the detail on that bench. It was worth the trip just to see this place." Smiling, I cannot wait to tell Gino.

CHAPTER 9

IT HAS BEEN A week since I broke down at Gino's shop, and since then I have been back three times. Going to his shop was the best thing I could have done for us. Even though I did break down in front of him, it opened a new side to our relationship. I would not have thought that possible after fifteen years of marriage. We have always been open and honest in our relationship, and while we would do anything for each other, we slowly fell into a comfortable routine and stopped challenging one another to grow and take chances. Each of us was hurting, and neither of us realized it. *Hurting* might be too strong of a word, but over the years we made assumptions instead of asking each other what we wanted. Secretly, we were emotionally stuck, happy with each other but not with our lives. Perhaps Gino was happy, but he could have been happier.

I never thought my struggles could affect both of us. I suppose if I had thought about it, I would have considered that, but being so wrapped up in my world, I did not. Ironically, if I were still working at the bank, I do not think I would have these realizations. Would we have continued living the way we have been all these years? Would something drastic have happened to wake me up from my living coma? I will never know the answer, but at least now my eyes are opened to my hurt and the hurt I unintentionally caused, and I can do something about it.

Going to the shop almost makes me feel like we're dating again and seeing each other in a new way. Business is good because of the holiday draw, so I have been helping Gino by working the register and showing customers around. The spirit in the air is miraculous. Everyone is happy, and the mood is contagious. The shops are glowing with their Christmas décor, drawing large crowds from neighboring towns and villages, and we have even had a few light dustings of snow to set the mood. I am caught up in the full spirit of the season.

This time the weatherman got it right. It is after ten in the morning the following day and Gino and I are in the kitchen enjoying a nice lazy Christmas Eve morning brunch. Wrapped in my warm robe, wearing my favorite slippers, and holding a mug of coffee in my hands, I lean back against the kitchen counter. It is such a perfect morning, the three of us here. My heart is so happy I feel like I could not be any happier. Luigi is curled up in the corner of the kitchen. His head is resting gently on his right paw, but his eyes are quietly observing in case some culinary treat should find its way to his section of the kitchen. He looks so content. I am watching Gino make breakfast. He is the better chef in the house.

While I prefer to bake, Gino has a familial culinary gift that has been passed down through generations. Closing my eyes and immersing myself in the moment, I am consumed with the smells wafting around the kitchen. Crispy bacon frying on the stove, freshly made coffee, a ham quiche in the oven—but the part that makes my mouth water is the streusel coffee cake on the table. I confess it is not homemade, but it sure looks delectable. I bought it yesterday on Main Street. The bakery smelled too good to pass up, and once I set foot inside, I passed the point of no return. The result of my unplanned stop helped make our Christmas Eve breakfast all the tastier.

"Babe, look out the window," Gino says. I shake myself out of my food fantasy and walk over to join him at the kitchen window.

Everything is blanketed with snow. It looked like a Norman Rockwell painting. "Oh, it's beautiful. I wondered when it was going to start. I heard last night they are calling for close to twenty-six inches."

"I think we will be here for quite some time if that's what they expect. You know how long it takes the plows to clear the roads. I think today will be a great snow day. Let's eat," Gino says as he grabs two plates and heads to the stove.

After feeling like I had been run over by multiple trucks over the last six months, I am more than ready for a relaxed Christmas season with Gino. We spend time together and talk about things we have not talked about in years: our future, our hopes and wishes, where we see us in five years, what changes we want to make, and what trips we want to take. The list is endless, and it is the first in a while that Gino and I have had such deep, personal conversations. After all these years of married life, I see Gino differently. We've both grown in our respective lives but have not grown together. Thinking about how long it has taken us to reach this point, I am glad the time has finally come. We need this if we want to continue this new path to a harmonious relationship with one another. I am tired of passing time and being mildly okay with where I am. It is time to make the changes we want to create for ourselves.

Without a doubt, we have always been happy together, and that will never change—but if there is a way that we can be even happier, why not strive for that? We agree to use the winter to discuss this and devise with a plan. While many instigators led us to this admission, the new year seems like the perfect time to begin the process.

Come February and March, Gino's business was still in high demand. I started working with him regularly about three days a week, so he did not have to hire help. It worked out perfectly, and I love every minute of it. We spend more time together, and I get to see him in action, where he is most happy, creating. We both stay busy, and because of the constant flow of phone calls and customers, we often go a good part of the day without seeing each other. For the first time, I see the business as our business, giving me purpose, hope, and direction. I have a reason to get up in the morning. I have something to look forward to. And I can see the results of our hard work: Gino on the creative side and me on the marketing and financial sides. It is a great feeling. I do not know why neither of us saw this as an option in the beginning, but I am thankful that we recognize it now. Working independently yet together has strengthened our connection, and we finally recognize the value that each of us brings to our relationship on many levels.

CHAPTER 10

WHILE I LOVE WORKING at the shop with Gino, I have finally begun to treasure the days I am home. I have fallen into an easy routine of walking, coffee, and working at the computer on the mornings I am off. I'm working on my journal rewrites again. Recently, my time has become more valuable to me. In the quiet and solitude of home, I sit at the kitchen table and read through the many pages of notes from that passionate summer many years ago. When I start to type, my fingers move fast, and I occasionally stop to collect my thoughts and reflect on the memories. I continue until my mind and fingers need a break. Then I re-read what I've written, making me want to keep going. Sometimes I go for hours. The feeling is intoxicating to me. I'm almost obsessed with writing our love story. Knowing that our love story is still in progress, I feel so lucky. I also find that writing has become a form of therapy for me. When I'm writing, I am not worried about my struggles because I don't seem to have any. I forget about the things I cannot control. I also feel like my writing has a purpose. It gives me a sense of fulfillment I have not felt in quite some time.

Even as fast as I'm typing, I have a hard time keeping up with my racing mind. I've been concentrating so hard that I feel like I have been running a marathon; my fingers are starting to cramp. Yet I'm thriving on my newfound hobby and how good it makes me feel, and I have to compel myself to stop and catch my breath. I look at the bottom of the screen to see how many pages I have pulled together over the last few months. Seventy-eight!

When I hear the phone ring, I'm happy for a reason to break away from the screen. I stretch my arms up to the sky, then push the chair back from the table and walk over to the phone.

"Hello?"

"Hi, Fran. Good morning! Is this a good time to chat?" Jane asks. "I didn't want to call too early, but I haven't talked to you in ages."

"Jane, I'm so happy to hear from you! It has been a while. I'm sorry I haven't picked up the phone sooner to call you. How are you feeling? Are the kids ready for their new baby brother or sister?"

"Oh, everyone is over the moon. We can't wait. The kids have names picked out already, and it's pretty much a waiting game now. The doctor says middle to end of July, and everything looks good."

"That's fantastic news."

"What about you? How are you doing?"

"Good, actually. I'm feeling pretty good. So, Gino and I have been talking a lot since the holidays, and it's been good. We agree we need to make some changes. We aren't sure what or how, but we're going to take the winter to discuss what we want to do. I can honestly say now that being laid off from the bank was the best thing for me. For us. I wouldn't have said that a few months ago, but now I'm starting to see that it opened my eyes to a lot of things, and I'm not afraid. In retrospect, I was content there but not happy. Maybe I was happy but not truly happy. Does that make sense?"

"Absolutely," Jane said.

"I feel like I was fine then, but now I want more of something and I'm not sure what. I can't go back to how things have been with my professional life. It's not fulfilling to me anymore. I need to move forward and be excited about what's to come. I'm not sure what that will be."

"I think that's a wise evaluation. No, I think that's a great evaluation. It's giving you time to look at new opportunities."

Something I have always admired about Jane is that she is a great listener. She always lets me talk things through before she adds her comments.

Laughing, I tell Jane, "You know, you should have been a shrink instead of an editor."

"Funny, Charlie tells me that whenever I tell him it's time to talk about us. I have to say that because, otherwise I don't know what he is thinking. He says I can read his mind. I say that's because he's an open book."

"You guys are the cutest couple I know," I say.

"So, what else have you been doing?"

"Well, I've been helping Gino at the shop a few days a week."

"Really! Are you enjoying that?"

"Yes, it's been great. But I've recently taken up a new hobby and love it more than I ever dreamed I would."

"Well, now you have me curious. What is this new hobby?" Jane asks.

"Do you remember that journal of notes I kept the summer we went to Italy?"

"Of course. You wrote in it all the time. You kept saying you wanted to remember every detail and how you felt.

"Well, back in October I found my notes. I was doing some searching on the computer, and I saw the file. They are just notes—bullet points. One day I looked at it again and started typing it into a story. I hadn't planned to do it, but once I started writing, I didn't want to stop. I get so excited at the thought of what's materializing on the pages. I have my notes to guide me, and most of it is accurate, but it's been a long time, so I've reimagined some of the details. I'm not sure what to do with it, but I've enjoyed it. I haven't even told Gino about it. I haven't told anyone except you."

"That's amazing, Fran! How many pages do you have already?"

So excited and still shocked by the number I shout into the phone, "Seventy-eight! I can't believe it. And I'm not even halfway."

"Send it to me," Jane says.

"What? No, it's just something I've been working on for fun. I'm not sure I want anyone to read it."

"Really, Fran. Send it to me. You may have found your calling. Maybe this is what you have been searching for all this time. I mean, think about it. You wouldn't have stumbled on it if you had worked at the bank. You said you are so happy and excited when writing. You sound happier than you've sounded in months. This is what I do. Let me read it and give you my honest thoughts. If it's nothing, you have nothing to lose, but if it's something, then maybe this is your path. You aren't going to find what you are looking for if you don't put forth the effort. Why not be open to possibility?"

"Okay, let me think about it. I guess it would be amazing if you thought it was good. I don't want to get too excited about something and have it taken away from me. Right now, it's mine and mine alone. It's my world to escape to. If someone tells me it isn't good, I'm afraid it may not hold the same meaning for me anymore. I've been grasping for something for far too long. I don't want it taken away from me. Not yet."

"I understand. That is worth consideration. But remember, you don't get anywhere without opening yourself to new possibilities and challenges. Listen, all I ask is that you think about it. Maybe not today; maybe not tomorrow, but when you are ready, I am here. Speaking of work, I must run, but I'm serious. Think about it and keep me posted."

"I will—and, Jane, thank you for hearing me. I mean it. I'm so thankful I have a good friend like you in my life." And with that, we both hang up.

It's true what Jane said about opening to new possibilities. I know I should, but in my heart, I do not know if I can take rejection. I have worked hard over the years trying to find what I am good at, and I have not been too successful at finding it until now. I have finally found something that is mine: if nothing else, I have my words, my writing, to escape to. It's important to me, and that's enough. But, sitting at the table, staring at the screen, a small part of me wonders. What if it is good? What if someone wanted to publish it and make it a book? Is that possible? It never crossed my mind. Would someone care to read it? Even if one person can enjoy the words I have strung together, maybe I need to be open to new possibilities and stop being afraid. At least I would have something to show for myself. All this time I have spent at home would be for a reason. Instead of wasting away, waiting for things to come to me, I would make my dreams happen.

Recently I have realized that I overanalyze situations. I have a way of sabotaging my happiness. Instead of appreciating opportunities as the gifts they are, I always find an excuse to bow out. But why? Why is it always right for someone else but not for me? Why is it so easy to pull back instead of jumping in?

Needing some time to clear my head and erase my self-deprecating thoughts, I call out to Luigi to go for a walk. I have always been a regular walker, and now I feel like I need one more than ever. It is still cold out for the beginning of March, so I bundle up before grabbing Luigi's harness and leash, and we head out the door.

The cold is refreshing and energizing to me, and I know Luigi loves it since he is always bundled in fur. And I am ready for warmer weather, especially after all the snow we have had this year. Even though it is damp and overcast today, I smile at the thought of the warm sun covering my face like a blanket as I stare up at the sky, mesmerized by the purest blue. I take Luigi up the path to the open field by our house. The walk is so familiar—my legs are on autopilot and my mind can drift. I have always been fascinated with the workings of the mind, and this is one of those moments that invokes my wonderment. I am not thinking of anything in particular; it's more like tidbits of everything. Seemingly random thoughts last seconds, yet they form complete conversations in my head. It's amazing how so much information can form in your mind in the time it takes to snap your fingers.

I recall the conversation that Jane and I had minutes ago. A feeling of excitement bubbles up in my belly. What if this could happen? What if I could be a writer? I never want to return to working at a bank, and I do not think I can handle a desk job now. I have grown accustomed to doing things on my schedule. And ever since I started working with Gino part-time and writing on my off days, I feel whole. I feel like I have a reason to be, instead of waking up every morning longing to go to bed. Thinking about that, I am stunned. The time leading up to the holidays was hard, but when we had the party and company, I got so wrapped up in hosting that I did not have time to think of anything else. Right after the holidays, I transitioned into this new writing rhythm and spending time at the shop. It's been months since I wanted to go to sleep for the sole purpose of forgetting my thoughts.

And just like that, I stop dead in my tracks. Immediately my mind races uncontrollably. Thinking that my writing will lead to something more than a journal is a fantasy. I am not a writer. Why am I even spending my time on something that will not make a difference in my life?

Frustrated at the feelings I have allowed to creep up, I walk faster until I am almost at a jog. Luigi looks up strangely at me as he stays by my side. I say a prayer in my head. It is the only thing I know that will quell my disturbing thoughts and bring me back to some sense of peace. I have been feeling so good about myself lately. I have had purpose and hope. Why do I do this to myself? Sabotaging my thoughts and dreams before allowing them to happen is typical yet automatic for me. *I cannot fall back into this hole of despair. I will not let myself. God, please hear my prayers.*

When we finally get back to the house, I am not surprised that we were out for nearly two hours. To keep my ominous thoughts at bay, I must have unintentionally picked the longest route. Maybe I thought I could outrun my ominous thoughts, but I do not think that is ever likely. At most, I can distract myself from them for a while. In the end, they always win out.

Back inside, Luigi runs to his usual spot in the living room as I take off my hat and coat. Sweat is trickling down my back, and my hair is pasted to my head. Now that I'm not moving, a feeling of cold sets in quickly, so I take a shower to get warm and—if I'm lucky—reset my mood.

The warmth of the water coursing over my body acts like an eraser. My awful thoughts run down the drain along with the water. Feeling better and warmer but still cold, I search for something comfy. I put on a clean pair of jeans, my favorite soft-as-a-bunny light cream sweater, and my slippers. By the time I get downstairs, it is close to four o'clock, and I have not had anything to eat since the early morning. *No wonder I'm so hungry,* I think. I don't want to spoil my appetite for dinner, so I fix myself a snack of apples and peanut butter and make a cup of tea. With food on my mind, I plan dinner: maybe pasta with garlic bread tonight.

But what should I do until dinner? Part of me wants to sit at the computer and immerse myself in my writing. But I am afraid that if I start typing, I might think about the earlier conversation with Jane. I just cleared my head; the last thing I want to do now is invite all that self-doubt back into my head and risk projecting it onto Gino when he gets home. So I toss aside the idea of working on my journal this afternoon. My attitude is in sync with the weather: cold and drab. It is late in the day to start any big projects. So I pull a book off the bookshelf, grab my tea, and head for the living room. I start a fire in the fireplace, then curl up on the couch with a blanket and read.

A few hours later I hear Luigi dancing uncontrollably in the foyer. Gino is home. I must have dozed off; looking at the book in my lap, I notice I'm only a few pages in. Luigi's tail is tapping frantically against the floor, indicating he will not stop until he receives some attention, ideally in the form of a belly rub. Listening to Gino laugh, I smile and push the blanket off my lap. I glance at the clock to see it is after seven. The fire needs another log, but it's still burning enough to surround me with a pocket of warm air. As I stand up, the fire's warmth gives way to the cool air from the front hall. Gino walks in. The sight of him always takes my breath away, and as he walks over to give me a kiss, I think, *what a wonderful man I have.*

CHAPTER 11

IT IS NEARING THE end of March. While I have been enjoying my new routine of working at the shop with Gino and writing, I feel that progress on our agreement has stalled. We had said we would take the winter to figure out our plan. We have brainstormed, but we still have not made any significant changes, at least nothing that will make a permanent difference in our lives. Nothing has changed since before the holidays, and I cannot see change on the horizon. I am afraid that without something to propel me forward, I'm going to lose the progress I have made.

I do not think Gino is unhappy with his situation; however, things have been the same for him for the last fifteen years. For that reason alone, I suspect he could be happier. He works six days a week, has dinner, heads to bed when he starts to fall asleep on the couch and starts all over again the next day. It's wonderful that he devotes so much time to the shop, but he spends so much time there that he does not have a chance to enjoy the simple moments in life. Maybe I am jealous that he has something he cares about so passionately or that he doesn't have more time to spend with me. Still, I wonder if he works so hard that he does not see what he's missing.

Although I have been trying to find my path and have a purpose in my life, it is more important now than ever for us to grow as a couple. It cannot be about me finding my way and Gino finding his. A marriage is a couple growing together, each strengthening the other. I recognize this is not something I can do alone. I have the nagging feeling that there is something more out there for us, and while we have been searching the universe for answers, I am still waiting for a reply. I can feel my frustration mounting. Something has to change, and it needs to start now.

It is ten in the morning on a Tuesday, Gino is at work, and I am at the kitchen table working on the computer in what has become my usual spot. Having dedicated the first several hours of the morning to my writing, I am satisfied with my progress today. As I take a sip of my coffee, the phone rings.

"Hello?"

"Hey, babe. How's your morning going?"

"Hi, honey. Good. I'm working on the computer. I'm going to take Luigi out in a few minutes. How are you?"

"Good. Listen, I thought I would leave work early tonight. I should be home around five. Can I take you out for dinner? We could head up to Ruby's for burgers and shakes."

"That sounds great. We haven't had Ruby's in ages. Is it a slow day?" I ask.

"Yes, it is, but that's not why I'm closing early. You know how we have been talking the last few months about making changes?"

"Yes," I say cautiously.

"Well, I know you might be thinking that I have forgotten about what we've talked about, but on the contrary, I think about it every day. I haven't talked much about it because I haven't figured out any answers, and I know that's not what we had planned, especially this late in the season. We gave ourselves the winter to come up with ideas, and I know that's passing quickly. But, while I was working today, I had a thought. I want to talk with you about it tonight. Does that sound good?"

"I think it's great. Am I going to like it?"

"You are going to love it. I'll be home soon, and we can hash it all out tonight. I love you."

"I love you, too."

Setting the handset back on the cradle, I feel a little anticipation sneak into my thoughts as I speculate about this idea he wants to discuss. I know Gino hasn't forgotten about all our conversations at the start of the year. He probably doesn't know what changes to make or how to solve our dilemma. If neither of us knows, there is no point in bringing up the topic only to have it hang in the air with a heaviness that cannot be pushed away. Now more than ever, I want to rethink our conversations and be open to whatever Gino has in mind. Maybe this will be the start of a new future for us that will give us whatever we need. Whatever it is, change needs to happen.

I run a few errands to keep myself occupied. After I get home, Jane calls. It's a bit of a surprise because usually she calls before or after work because she tries to stay focused on her work schedule when she is in her groove.

However, it seems that, to her, the phone call is work-related. "Hey, Fran. So, have you thought more about sending me your work?"

"Honestly, I'm still not sure. I need a little more time to figure out some things. If this is all I have now, I don't want to lose it. I know that sounds funny. You would think anyone would jump at the opportunity for a publisher to look at their work, but what if it doesn't pan out?"

"You're right. Most people would jump at the opportunity. But remember what I told you earlier. You aren't going to find what you are looking for if you don't put forth the effort. In your case, you've already put forth the effort; you just have to hand it over. I'm not telling you what to do, but we've been friends for a long time. If you sit on it too long, you might never do it. I won't ask you again. I want you to think about it. I've got another call to make, but keep me posted, okay?"

I didn't even get a chance to say goodbye before the call disconnected. I know Jane is right. She's known me for a long time. It is easier for friends to see things in us than for us to notice them ourselves. Friends are impartial onlookers with nothing to lose and nothing to gain. They see what looks to them like the most obvious solution. I realize then that instead of learning to be strong in my convictions, I have become weak and helpless. I resolve to make this change. Maybe this is the one step I need.

It is almost four-fifteen when I get off the phone with Jane. I decide to run upstairs and jump in the shower before Gino gets home. This is the first time in a while he has closed early, and I know that spending time together means as much to him as it does to me. I want to be ready.

I come downstairs at ten minutes to five, just as the front door swings open. Gino and Luigi greet me at the bottom of the stairs. Smiling, Gino gives me a warm embrace and a kiss. "You look beautiful tonight."

Blushing for the first time in a while, I hide a grin. Taking the compliment as intended, I look up at Gino's smiling face and say, "Thank you."

"Are you ready for dinner?" Gino asks. "I'm starving."

"Yes," I say as I open the hall closet door, searching for my favorite brown clogs. I love the sound of clogs on a wood floor and how tall they make me feel. And I love the convenience—clogs are a quick way to feel more put-together.

Walking the front path to the car, Gino gets ahead of me and opens the passenger-side door. He always performs this lovely gesture for me, and, whether he knows it, it makes me feel special. The simple chivalrous act after all these years of marriage does a lot for my psyche. I think to myself that I probably should tell him that more often. This time, instead of thinking it, I turn to Gino before stepping into the car and tell him.

"Thank you for making me feel so special when you open the car door. And when you pull out a chair for me or bring me a cup of coffee with lots of cream and three sugars, or when you search for my hand to hold in yours. I don't tell you that enough. I wanted you to know."

I feel relieved. I don't express those feelings often enough, and I'm glad I remembered to say them this time. Gino is speechless, but the delighted look on his face is thanks enough. On the drive to the diner, I can see out of the corner of my eye the grin on Gino's face. It also makes me grin, knowing he is happy with me next to him. While we have had our talks over the last few months—and I had my breakdown in his shop that time and let some feelings out—this felt different. It felt whole, sweet, and good, and the mixed emotions was mutual, not just mine.

For the next twenty minutes, we ride in silence together. It is a comfortable quiet that doesn't need to be filled with words or music. I have noticed that few spouses have the skill or desire to practice this form of communion. I regard it as a sanctuary. I find comfort in being in the quiet company of the one I love, knowing there is no need for anything but being present.

Gino pulls into a parking space at Ruby's. I notice it is not as busy as normal, but it is a Tuesday evening. I am glad not to have a crowd. Walking into the diner, we see a few people we know and exchange pleasantries. Gino sees a few customers from his shop and stops to say hello. Ruby, the owner, sees us and comes speeding over, hugging us and showing us to our favorite booth. We do not get here as often as we would like since it is not close to home, but in years past, we were frequent customers and developed a close friendship with Ruby and her husband, George. They came to the house for our Thanksgiving celebration.

"I'm so happy to see y'all. You made my evening. What can I get you?" Ruby asks.

Whenever Ruby talks, I think of Flo from the old television show *Alice*. She has big puffy hair like Dolly Parton and a long Southern drawl. She makes you feel like family the moment she starts talking. It is a skill, and she sure has it down because you always feel good about yourself when you leave. That always brought us back to the diner—and the Oreo milkshakes. I also love the décor here. It's not put on; it's original. Ruby's has been around a long time, and no other place in the area can match its classic charm. The waitresses even wear pink uniforms with white aprons. The uniforms turn some people off, but it adds to the ambiance. As we take off our coats and slide into the vintage booth, Gino says to Ruby, "Make it the usual."

Ruby smiles and writes it on her notepad. "That's two cheeseburgers with fries and two Oreo milkshakes. You got it. I'll leave you two lovebirds and be back in a few minutes with your shakes."

"Thank you, Ruby," we say in unison. Barely unable to keep my excitement contained any longer, I am about to ask Gino what his idea is when George, Ruby's husband, walks by the table. Seeing my face fall, Gino gives me a wink.

"I hope I'm not interrupting anything. I saw you two walk in and wanted to say hello," George says, sounding like Wilford Brimley. Come to think of it, he kind of looks like him too.

"Not at all, George. It's a pleasure as always to see you. We came for the best burgers and Oreo shakes in the area. No place else compares," Gino says proudly.

George laughs at Gino's enthusiasm, saying, "This is why we love you guys. Great to see you. Enjoy your food. Let us know if we can get you anything else."

George and Gino shake hands again, and George turns to me with a smile before walking away.

Gino looks at me and reaches across the table for my hands. Holding them, he moves his thumbs in circles, then bends his head as if deep in thought. Grinning, he looks at me and says, "Fran, you are like a kid on Christmas morning. I can see the anticipation is eating you up inside."

"Would you just tell me already," I blurt out a little too loudly and we both chuckle at my eagerness.

"Okay, okay. You have been patient long enough. So, as I told you on the phone, I have been giving our talks a lot of thought over the last few months. I know I don't always voice my opinion so openly, but I think it's because with this situation, I don't know what the answer is. I don't know how to fix it. I feel like I have failed you in that regard."

I shake my head.

"I know losing your job has been hard for you and I'm sorry that I haven't helped you in ways that I wish I could. As much as it has bothered you it has bothered me too, knowing that I can't help you. I think like you, only it's taken me quite a bit longer to realize it, we have been kind of in a rut, and I don't mean that in a bad way, just that things have gotten routine. I love my work and I love you. I have my two favorite things in the world right here with me. When I immerse myself in what's important to me, I block out the rest of the world. The difference is that I didn't see how my doing that only made you more unhappy."

As he finishes his last sentence Ruby comes to the table with a basket of fries and the Oreo milkshakes. Setting the fries on the table, Ruby says, "You both look so deep in conversation I almost didn't want to disturb you. Here are your shakes and the fries. The burgers will be right up."

The fries smell so good that my mouth waters. "Mmm! Ruby, the fries smell great, but that milkshake looks divine," I say, devouring them with my eyes.

"Extra thick and lots of cookies, just the way you like it. Enjoy. I'll be back in a few."

Unable to wait, Gino and I dive into our shakes. Ruby's shakes are so thick you have to work hard for that first sip, but it's worth it. Sometimes you have to use a spoon because cookie pieces get stuck in the straw.

Gino starts to chuckle at my love for all things sweet. He pushes the basket of fries to me. "Have some."

"Delicious. But the shake is better. I could have this shake for dinner and be blissfully happy."

Taking one longer sip, we get back to the discussion. "Your dedication to your work doesn't make me unhappy," I tell Gino. "I'm thrilled that it makes you so happy. I want us to feel that same happiness too, only more. We've been comfortable for so long. I think it's time for us to change things up. I feel like we can be better. I know that's hard to explain. But I want us to do it together so we can both be excited."

Picking up a couple of fries, Gino says, "I get it and now that I am aware of it, I can't go back either. I can't go back to the way things have been. I don't want to. I want us to be happy together in whatever capacity that takes us."

Relieved to hear him say that and know we are on the same page regarding our feelings, Ruby stops by the table to bring our burgers.

"Those burgers look great," I say.

"Hot off the grill and just how you like 'em—cheddar cheese, lettuce, tomato, and hold the onions. I brought y'all some water too. Sometimes those fries can be a little salty. Can I get you anything else?" Ruby asks.

"Delicious. Thanks, Ruby," Gino says.

Gino and I take a bite of our burgers. "Oh, my gosh. This was such a great idea coming here tonight. This burger is so good," I say.

"I had no idea I was this hungry. It hit the spot," Gino says as he takes another bite of the burger. Wiping his mouth with the napkin from his lap, Gino picks the conversation back up. "So, while working this morning, I kept thinking about us and what's important to us. Do you remember the summer we met and how we spent the time driving around, exploring everything and sightseeing?"

Eager to hear him keep talking, I nod as I reach for another sip of my milkshake. I am excited knowing that he feels the way I do. I know in my heart something will change tonight. Maybe not for the long haul, but something will change to bridge us to where we need to go.

"We lived for each other and with minimal possessions. I don't know about you, but it was probably the best summer of my life. I loved how we enjoyed the simplest of things, yet they seemed so grand to us. I don't know if it was because we were so caught up in each other or if it was the timing, location, or melding of our lives but I know the feeling was insatiable and real."

Stopping to take a sip of water, he continues while leaning against the back of the booth. Watching him, I am studying him and realize that I haven't seen this side of Gino in quite some time. He is animated and excited. He is the man I married.

"We need to go back to Italy. We need to be reminded of what brought us together in the first place and why we need each other now more than ever. I am not looking to recreate the same memories of what we once had all those years ago. They were wonderful memories and ones we will never forget but we are two different people now from the kids we were back then. We've had a married life and life experiences together and maybe this is what we need to reset our compass," Gino says as he leans forward and takes another sip of his milkshake. "Besides, it would be great to see some family we haven't seen in a long time, and we haven't been on a vacation in years."

Not sure what I had expected, I sit back and think about what he said.

"I think it's a great idea. I don't know why we didn't think to do it years ago. Maybe this is why we are meant to do it now because all of this has led us to this moment."

"That's exactly my thoughts too. We are at the end of March. I thought we could leave in June. I need a few months to finish some of my orders, and I won't take any more until we get back. Business has been so good the last several years. I'm sure my regular clients will understand. If not, well, this is something we have to do. I'm sorry, Fran. I'm sorry that I never thought about this before and that it never occurred to me to let us take some time to escape reality if only to recharge. It's long overdue."

"Honey, you have nothing to be sorry about. We have nothing to be sorry about. It's the way life has taken us. Now that we know, we can do something about it. Who knows, maybe this trip will be the inspiration we need." Taking the last sip of what is left from the shake, I set the glass down and run a napkin across my lips. I feel satisfied. As I look up, Ruby comes by to clear our dishes.

"Y'all must've been hungry. There's not a drop left on either of your plates. That's what we like to see here, full bellies," Ruby says, smiling as she picks up the plates and glasses.

"Ruby, when you get a minute, we'll take the check, too," Gino says.

"Oh, no, not this time. This meal is on the house. It's our way of saying thank you for that wonderful Thanksgiving feast." Ruby turns to walk away before we can argue. Yelling behind her, she adds, "You two have a beautiful night!"

We both shout, "Thank you, Ruby," as she disappears behind the kitchen's swinging double doors.

We rise from the table and put on our coats. I turn around to see Gino scribbling a note on the back of the check and leaving a twenty. *Gino has such a soft heart*, I think, and I smile.

We walk to the car hand in hand. With my belly full but not stuffed and feeling happy about our conversation, I close my eyes and relax on the drive home. Finally, we have a plan. Maybe it is not the answer to our dilemma, but it is a start. Most important, it gives us the hope we need to move forward.

CHAPTER 12

It's funny how time has no boundary. It stays the same every hour, every minute, every second, yet our minds have the awesome ability to perceive it differently. Time does not change; we change. My mind has a silly way of making me think I have no time, yet I have lots of time. In fact, I probably have more time than most people. I think I have only thirty minutes to get ready because I do not want to be stuck in traffic. But even if it takes me an hour, where am I going after that? I am always racing against time. Sometimes I feel as if time rules my life. I must remind myself that time is not the enemy; it is what life is made of. I can embrace the present and know the breaths I take at this second are what is important, not the seconds on the clock yet to come. I need to learn to let the clench of the clock release its tight hold on me. I need to learn to accept being in the moment, to live today.

Sitting at the kitchen table, I open the laptop and pull up my journal. It is still early, but the sun is already shining brightly. I immerse myself in my world. I have not worked on it as much as I would have liked in the last several weeks, but I feel I am making good progress. A passage about Jane makes me pause to think about what she said the other day about sending her some of my writing. While I have talked to her a few times since then, she has held to her word and hasn't asked me again. Maybe I should send her a draft. Why be afraid? I feel like Gino and I are on the verge of something new. Maybe my writing is part of that.

"That's it. I'm not sitting on the sidelines anymore. I'm getting in the game," I say out loud. "If I'm going to do this, I'll need a title." I sit back in my chair and think, tapping my fingers on the table. After a few moments, the perfect title comes to mind. I add a blank page at the beginning of the document and type:

the start of it all
by francesca martinelli

"Yes, I like it. It's simple, and it's true. I'm starting new after graduation from college, and I have the whole world in front of me." I save the document, pull up my email, and write to Jane.

Jane,

I've been thinking a lot about what you said about my writing, and I have decided to take you up on your suggestion. Remember, it's not finished yet, but if you like it, then I will send the rest when it's done.

Which leads me to my next point for emailing you. Gino and I had a conversation last night. We decided to plan a trip to Italy. I'm so excited! Gino came up with the idea. He thought it would be a great time to get away for a while, visit family, recharge. And it will be a great place to write and think so I can wrap up my novel. I'll fill you in on the details later, but I know we will be leaving within a few days.

I owe you a lot, but mostly I want to thank you for always listening to me.

Love,

Fran

XO

I attach the file containing what I have written of the manuscript so far, then quickly hit "send" before I change my mind.

"There, it's done. I did it. Now I wait and see."

Still sitting at the computer, I daydream about what could be. I can feel the palpitations in my heart as I imagine different outcomes. Some of them I would rather not think about. Perhaps ten minutes later, as I push away from the table, I hear the ding indicating a new message. I pull my chair back up and open the email. It's a reply from Jane.

Fran,

I knew you would do it. I will pass it along, and we will go from there. Remember, every writer gets rejections, so whatever happens, it's just the beginning of your journey. We may not hear anything for a few months, so don't panic. Fingers crossed.

I can't wait to hear more details about the trip. We can take Luigi for you. Just let us know if there is anything else we can do.

Love,

Jane XO

I feel relieved that I just made a huge decision that had been weighing on me. I figure now is a good time to take a break in more ways than one. We have not been on vacation in years. We leave for Italy in a week. Our tickets are open-ended; maybe we'll stay a week, maybe a month. I have no pressing need to get back by a specific date, and Gino is closing the shop for the summer, so he's not too concerned, either. The thought of "going with the flow" is starting to shape how I think about my time. I'm excited about a change of pace.

Other than a few times with Gino over the last several months, today is the first time I have felt confident that things will work out. At least, I keep praying they will. I have to. Hope is the only thing keeping me moving forward.

CHAPTER 13

THIS DAY HAS FINALLY come. It seemed out of reach for so long, and the closer it got, the longer it took to arrive. I could hardly sleep last night. I think my anticipation and excitement for the trip have me on full alert to ensure I do everything I need to do before we leave. I can see daylight creeping around the sides of the shades. Unable to sleep anymore, I push the covers back, grab my robe and slippers, and tiptoe out of the room, with Luigi following. Gino is still sleeping, and although he is a heavy sleeper, it will be a long day and I do not want to wake him too early.

I start some coffee and let Luigi out. I realize it will be some time before I do this again. I hope Luigi does not think we are abandoning him. We have never left him this long before, but I feel better knowing he will be with Jane and her family. He will have his share of belly rubs and hugs from their kids. I would not be surprised if he sneaks away for some alone time, too.

While the coffee is brewing, I lean back against the counter and look around our kitchen. Thinking back over the last year, I realize how much time I have spent in this room, how many tears I have shed here, and how long I have sat at this table searching for something and feeling as if I might never find any answers. It would be unfair to say I was alone in my fight but fighting through the unbearable in your mind is a lonely business even when surrounded by loved ones. I have this strong, overwhelming feeling that whatever happens on this trip, something will change for us. I am not sure how it will happen or what it will be, but all I can do is pray and take each day in turn. Somehow, by some miracle, I have been okay lately, and I sense that this feeling will not only endure but change for the better in the coming months.

"Good morning, babe," Gino says, walking into the kitchen. He kisses me. "The coffee smells good. I just thought that it reminds me of the coffee we had at the café where we met. Man, that was some good stuff. I can't wait to get some when we get there."

"Definitely not grocery store brand," I say as I pull two mugs out of the cupboard.

"Hey, let's leave early for the airport," Gino says. "We can drop off Luigi first and then I want to swing by the shop one last time. We need to plan for about four hours. I'm not sure how traffic will be heading into the city." Then he puts his arms around me in a warm embrace. "I know how excited you are about this trip. I am, too. Remember, Fran; there is no going back to how things have been. I think we both realize that now. We will find a way to make some changes. I know it's going to be good. We are in this together."

"I know. I have this overwhelming feeling something good will happen for us. I can feel it," I say excitedly. "And Gino, I love you." I feel safe in his arms, and while I could stay here all day, I know we don't have much time. "I'm going to go take a shower and get dressed. I'll be ready soon."

As I'm heading toward the stairs, Gino calls after me. "I love you too, Fran, more than you can possibly know."

I look at his handsome face as he pours coffee into his mug. He looks at me and smiles.

Hours later, after making all our stops, saying goodbye to Jane, Charlie, and Luigi, and making Jane promise to call us the moment she heads to the hospital, we are finally on our way to the airport. I will miss Jane immensely, and I'm sad that I might not be with her when she has her baby, but I will miss Luigi most of all. I will miss his fluffy, furry head peeking over the edge of the bed when I open my eyes in the morning. I will miss our morning walks, the funny way he tilts his head as if he has a question, and most of all, giving him belly rubs. I will surely miss him fiercely, so I am as excited to get home as I am to go.

The flights to Munich and Genoa are not crowded, uncommon for this time of year. We hit the sweet spot after the college kids head out for their summer breaks and before the school year has ended for families with younger kids. Even the layover in Munich isn't bad; the four hours pass quickly.

Landing in Genoa brings back a flood of memories. The last time I was here was right after college graduation with my friends. It was the trip of a lifetime and one that changed my life. Thinking about it now, this trip might change my life too. Now, more than ever, I feel as if I am on a mission, one I cannot afford to let fail.

As we exit the jetway and step into the gate area, we are met with the sight of a crowd spread out before us, waiting to board the plane we emptied. More passengers are deplaning behind us, so we step to one side. I set my bags down long enough to take off my blue cardigan and tie it around my waist. Once I have adjusted my purse across my torso and gotten a better grip on my heavy leather carry-on bag, we rejoin the stream of travelers on their way to customs and the baggage claim. People are scrambling everywhere, trying to get to their gate on time, find their waiting party, squeeze in one last trip to the newsstand, or myriad other scenarios I can only imagine. Multiple loudspeakers are announcing names, flight numbers, and gate numbers, first in Italian and then in English, overlapping each other to the point that it takes great concentration to decipher which announcement, if any, applies to you. It is a constant flow of noise. I want to catch my breath and savor the realization that we are here, but I have only a moment to pull my heavy leather bag over my shoulder and make sure my sweater is still tied to me before Gino gently pulls me toward the baggage claim.

There is a thrill in traveling, but there is an even bigger one when you travel to other countries. The new sounds are endless. Routines and rituals of different cultures mingle, and the diversity of languages spoken is captivating. As Gino and I walk the concourse, I cannot help but wonder where everyone else is going and why. Are they traveling for work or visiting family and friends? Are they taking a vacation or maybe headed to a romantic rendezvous? All these people making their way somewhere to meet up with someone, surprise someone, touch base, catch up, get away, or come home—I smile at the possibilities.

People line the baggage carousel three or four deep on all sides. We shimmy our way in and around the crowd until finally we spot our two bags and pull them off the belt.

Next we look for a kiosk to get directions to the rental car. Fortunately, they aren't far. The thought of dragging these bags down another long corridor does not appeal to me. Not that I couldn't do it, but the crowd is too thick. I have already seen a few tense exchanges along the way, and I do not want to be included in one.

I laugh when I see the coffee shop around the corner from the rental car counters. It is the same shop where my friends and I stopped for espressos after arriving here fifteen years ago. We had been up all night at a party before our flight and drank way too many espressos that morning. As a result, we were beyond wired the rest of the day and didn't sleep on the plane. Of course, once we got to Genoa, we felt we needed a little pick-me-up before leaving the airport to carry us through the rest of the morning. It did not help that we stopped in a few towns on our way from the airport to our hotel, and each of them had a coffee shop. By the time we checked in at the hotel that evening, we had been going nonstop for over thirty-six hours, and we crashed hard on the hotel beds before we could even take off our shoes. Traveling is different when you are young, free, and ready to see the world. I am still young, but I am also more responsible. I know my limits.

With our bags packed in the trunk of the rental car, we start the next leg of our journey, the drive to Portofino. I look over at Gino in the driver's seat. He looks so content weaving in and out of airport traffic, knowing exactly where to go and what the signs say. It is as if he never left Italy, even though he is more American now than Italian—but I suppose your true roots never leave you. He fits right in with this world. The honking of car horns does not aggravate people here as it does in the

States. In Italy, honking at another driver is more like saying "hello" than shaking a fist. It is a rather comical experience and one you must see to understand its irony. People seem calmer here. They're in a hurry, but it is a slow hurry as if they have all the time in the world. It is a far cry from the world Gino and I just left.

It is just after three-thirty in the afternoon by the time we are out of the city. I can't contain my excitement any longer; I let out a whoop, and Gino laughs and cheers. After all these years, we are back in Italy together, sharing another adventure in the place where it all began. Even though the day has been long with travel and we both feel the toll of jet lag creeping in, Gino decides to drive along the magnificent Mediterranean coastline, also known as the Italian Riviera. I haven't quite taken in the reality of everything until now. Looking around at the cars, the landscape, the buildings, and the people, I am immediately released from all my worries and stress. It is as if I have been transported out of my body and there is nothing to hold me down. I roll down my window and take a deep breath of the ocean air.

The sheer beauty of this land is astounding. Bordered by the sea, the Alps, and the Apennine Mountains—France to the west, Tuscany to the east—it could not get any better. In my head, I say a quiet prayer. I pray for direction, inspiration, and us. Surely the beauty of this landscape is too extraordinary not to have been helped along by the hand of God. What better place to be closer to Him than a place that feels like heaven?

Gino is getting more and more excited as he points out historic landmarks, famous buildings, town names on signs, and the beauty of the sea meeting the rocks along the coastline.

I am excited for him. I cannot imagine what it's like to live far from the country of one's birth. Gino has told me many stories about growing up in Italy and learning the woodworking trade from his grandfather. I am sure this homecoming is stirring up a lot of memories and feelings. I think he loved it here, and he probably would have given just about anything to return, but his life and his family were elsewhere by then, and to him, that won out.

Like the last time I was here, I want to remember everything. I want to remember the smells, tastes, scenery, and experiences, and I want to remember how they made me feel. After years of trying to figure out life and how to live it, I do not want to spoil this experience by thinking of the past or the future. I want to be here, today, in the present, knowing I am happy with who I am and spending this moment with the man I love.

We spend the afternoon blissfully, driving and occasionally pulling off into parking areas along the shoreline. The freedom of having nowhere to be and no timetable to meet is priceless. I am learning to let time be measured by the light in the sky and not by the positions of the hands on a clock. Remembering my conversation with myself only weeks ago, I am keeping true to myself and not letting time rule my world.

Gino and I walk hand in hand along the beach, taking in the unimaginable beauty of this place. It is so moving to my spirit; it is like listening to an inspiring piece of music so commanding it brings tears to my eyes. I am always amazed at the power of a sight or sound to generate a storm of emotions in the body. Those emotions take root now.

We simply go with the flow and take in the seconds as they unroll before us. The many sensations we experience start to mix with a little exhaustion. By the time we reach the city limits of Portofino, it is already closing in on eight in the evening. Neither of us wants to succumb to our fatigue but keeping our eyes open is getting harder.

"Let's grab a pizza and call it a night," Gino says as we near the hotel. "We can start fresh in the morning."

Nodding in agreement, I say, "Yeah, I don't know how much longer I can keep my head up. That sounds like a great idea."

By the time we walk into the hotel, talk to the clerk, and arrive in our room, I am so tired that I could have walked into a Super 8 motel and thought it was the Ritz-Carlton. I have never been so happy to have a bed. As soon as my head hits the pillow, I fall into a much-needed sleep.

CHAPTER 14

THE NEXT MORNING, I wake up in the most comfortable bed
with sheets so soft I feel like I am lying on velvet. For a moment
I cannot remember where I am, and then I open my eyes and
see Gino lying beside me, still asleep and oblivious. I stretch
my arms above my head and my toes to the edge of the bed.
I'm in no rush to get up, yet I can feel the start of a dialogue in
my head: melt into this comfortable bed, or see the balcony?
Like a kid ready to eat a glazed chocolate donut on a Sunday
morning, I gingerly shimmy my way out of bed to not disturb
Gino. It is still dark in the room; I can see only one blinding
strip of light coming in below the edge of the rouladen that
is not fully closed. I fumble for my suitcase and feel around
inside for a robe to slip over my shirt. I find it and slip into the
bathroom.

I press my palm against the wall, but there is no light switch.
Then I remember that light switches in Europe are placed outside
the entryway to the room instead of inside. I backtrack and slide
my hand up the wall outside the door to the bathroom. When I
feel the switch, I quickly press it, step inside the bathroom, and
silently close the door before the light wakes Gino. My jaw drops

at the beauty of this rather large room. I think surely we have made a huge mistake. The bathroom floor is heated tile marble. There is a gold chandelier above my head with so many icicles that you would think it is winter. The shower is the size of our laundry room at home and has five showerheads and a bench on each side. The sink is a beautiful marble that matches the floor and is so wide and deep one could probably take a bath in it. I have never seen a room this elegant and beautiful—and this is only the bathroom. What must the view from the terrace be like? I quietly open the bathroom door, tiptoe my way to the balcony door, and slip outside as quickly as I can so as not to wake Gino. The terrace is huge. It has a bistro table and two chairs and even has room to walk around.

Looking back toward our room, I see that the balcony entrance is not one door but a set of double doors, no doubt designed to frame the beautiful view of the water when one is inside. The balcony spindles are made of wrought iron. The view is majestic—as beautiful as anything we saw the day before. Peering down, I see water the color of jade. Black rocks—boulders—line the cove inlet on both sides, where the water curves around to merge with the sea. Tall trees and pastel-painted buildings line the colossal seaside cliffs. The town has not come to life yet, so boats of every size are bobbing at anchor on the choppy water, surrounded by sparkling reflections of sunlight. In the golden light of morning, the reflections look like flames dancing around the boats.

I lean forward and rest my forearms on the balcony railing. As I am taking it all in, I hear the door crack open behind me. Gino walks up behind me, wraps his arms around my waist, and kisses the top of my head.

"Good morning," he murmurs in my ear.

"I think we have landed in heaven."

He laughs. "I take it this hotel meets your approval?" I hear the gentle morning roughness in his voice.

"When you said you would take care of the hotel, I had no idea this is what you had in mind. I could get used to this." I turn around and hug him.

"It is pretty amazing, isn't it? It's even prettier than I remember. The owners are family friends. This place has been in their family for generations. They offered me a deal I could not pass up, and I knew you would have no complaints."

"This is just unbelievable. I have no words. I was so tired last night I barely remember walking into the hotel, let alone the room. When I got up this morning, I thought for a moment that I was in someone else's room!"

We sit at the bistro table to enjoy the view. I like being here with my husband and knowing that we have a history here together, that this is where we met. It feels special. Before we arrived, I was not quite sure how it would feel to be back: Special? No feeling at all? Or a bland feeling of trying to recreate what once was? Fortunately, the first feeling won out, and I was pleasantly relieved. Now it is time to start bringing our dreams to life, creating new memories to add to our collection rather than simply rehashing old ones.

I say to Gino: "I don't even know what time it is. Do you?"

"It was just after six when I looked at the clock." That is one thing nice about traveling from west to east. While jet lag is not fun, if you can power through that first day without sleeping, you can wake up early the next morning while it is still relatively quiet.

"Let's get dressed and go get a coffee and a pastry. I'm hungry. We could perhaps go to 'our' café," I say with a smile.

We head back into our room to get ready. As I open the shades, I am in awe of the room itself. Gone are the traditional hotel-room furnishings that I am used to: the simple wood headboard, the plain matching nightstands, the not-so-fancy dresser that doubles as a TV stand, and of course, the required overstuffed chair. Instead, I feel as if I am in a palace. The two-toned parquet floors have a rich elegance. At the foot of the bed is a cream-colored settee with gold-colored braided trim so pretty I'm afraid to sit on it. The walls and doors have white wainscoting, intricate moldings surrounding soft blue-gray panels, and the occasional gilt-framed mirror or painting of the seaside cliffs. Gold-colored doorknobs and tiebacks pop against the blue-gray and coordinate with the floral tapestry-print floor-length curtains.

My initial shock at the room's grandeur and my thoughts of "can we afford this" quickly evaporate, and I remember my determination to keep my mindset in the present. If Gino is okay with this, then I am okay with it. And besides, when was the last time we vacationed? We are here on a mission to forge a new and exciting path, and I will do everything in my power to make the mission succeed.

With such a luxurious hotel room, I would be perfectly fine staying in the room and watching the scene on the water play out. On the other hand, being in the presence of elegance, I also want to feel it. I pull out my suitcase and look for something to wear. I decide on a pastel blue floral-print dress with spaghetti straps and comes to my knees. I love this dress because it makes me feel pretty and alive, the same way a good pair of jeans can make one feel confident. I also love the way it flows. When I spin around, the skirt flares like a party dress. When I was a kid, I loved to wear dresses that spun wide when I twirled around. It is funny that I have never outgrown that fun feeling.

I put on my comfortable walking sandals (maybe Gino can take me dancing later and I can wear my dancing shoes). I comb my hair and add a touch of lipstick, then put on my cream-colored silk wrap to keep the morning chill off until the sun has a chance to spread its warmth.

I tell Gino I am ready. He has been patiently waiting on the balcony, but given the location, the view, and our not having a schedule, he has no problem with the delay.

He extends his left elbow and says, "Fran, you look beautiful. Shall we?"

"Thank you." I am happy to hear the compliment, knowing he means it and is not saying it. I slide my right arm into his left and grab my purse as we walk out the door.

It is the perfect morning. The temperature is in the high seventies, but the humidity is low, so there is still a slight chill in the air. The sky is a brilliant blue with clouds so white and puffy they look like sheep that someone has meticulously arranged up high.

Only now, outside in the sunshine, do I realize the true scale of the hotel's elegance. The enormous portico is reminiscent of a 1960s James Bond movie, with stunning landscapes and beautiful people. I can imagine Bond coming into view on the steps, surrounded by large concrete statues and gold lampposts, then standing there confidently in his suit, looking as debonair as any gentleman could until he is joined by a beautiful woman with even more of a presence. It is not just the hotel that makes the area luxurious but also the people. It is the way they carry themselves, the clothes they wear. In many tourist towns, tank tops, flip-flops, and cutoff shorts are the norm, but these tourists are as impeccably dressed as extras in a Hollywood movie.

Gino and I walk arm in arm to the café where we first met, admiring the architecture, the boats, and the landscape along the way. Most tourists have not begun venturing out yet, so we have our pick of seats. We find the spot we sat in all those years ago.

"This is even more beautiful than I remember," I say. "In some ways I feel like it was yesterday that I was here with you for the first time, but in other ways it all seems so new, too."

"I remember walking up here. I was on my way to my grandfather's shop. He had already sold it by then, but I was good friends with the new owner. As I passed, I looked over at the water to take in the awesome view and clear my head for a moment, but then I saw you. In the twenty seconds or so that I watched you, I decided I had to meet you and that's when I came over."

"I'm glad you did."

Taking my hand in his, Gino looks at me and smiles. "Fran, you are the most beautiful person I have ever met. I mean that in all ways: your mind, your beauty, your strength, and your desire to find yourself amid all your struggles. I'm glad we are here today, right now, with each other."

I know Gino supports me but hearing the words from his mouth makes me feel strong and formidable. "I think this trip is good for us. I think about that day all those years ago, and I wonder what my life would be like now if I hadn't come back here to find you. I love you so much, Gino. I know we say it every day. Those words are powerful and hearing and saying them is important to me. I love that you tell me and that you listen to me. I also want to thank you for supporting me and meeting me halfway on this venture. I love that we are doing it together."

We sit at the café all morning, lingering over lattes, reminiscing, people-watching, and sharing pastries.

Gino says, "Do you remember going to Camogli last time? We spent the day in and out of the shops and stuffing our faces with cannoli and ice cream."

"How can I forget? Everything looked and smelled so good I couldn't decide what I wanted to eat. Isn't that where we spent the day at the beach, too?"

"Yeah. Why don't we go there next?" Gino says.

"Sounds perfect."

We stand up, and Gino fishes in his pocket for some euros to leave on the table. Hand in hand, we walk back to the hotel to get the car, enjoying the sound of the surf in the distance.

The drive to Camogli from Portofino is short, but there is plenty of scenic beauty to appreciate along the way. Camogli is a gorgeous town—almost too pretty to be real. The colorful buildings are reminiscent of a mixed box of artists' pastels. They have ornate *trompe l'oeil* features, from cornices to balustrades and windows. When we park in the center of town and get out to walk around, I remember why I had so much fun visiting this place the last time. Restaurants, cafés, and artisans' shops are abundant. Each time you exit a shop, the rich aromas of basil, garlic, and sweet onion remind you that there is no shortage of good places to dine. Gino and I browse the shops full of creative and passionate work, in awe at the exquisite talent of the local artists. I pick out pieces here and there to bring home for friends and family—such as a vase that reminds me of Jane and her eclectic style. I like to give gifts that have a meaningful connection to the recipient. So when I shop, if I see something that reminds me of someone, I buy it. It might not be there if I come back later.

Occasionally we stop for gelato, coffee, or freshly baked baguettes. It is a perfect leisurely afternoon, with no place to rush to and no one waiting for us. When we return to the car to drop off our purchases, it is close to eight in the evening, and the temperature is beginning to drop along with the sun. I grab my wrap from the car, and we head to dinner at a restaurant overlooking the sea. Soon darkness will set in, and the streets will come to life with crowds of people laughing, drinking, and eating as if celebrating another day. For now, the sun is low on the horizon, casting its magnificent orange glow along the sea. It gives me the illusion that God is spreading His arms and hands out over the land as if to reward every person for a day well lived. As we sit at the restaurant enjoying the sounds of the people, the rush of the waves, the smell of the food, and the magic of day turning to night, Gino and I look at each other and, as if sharing the same thought, clink our glasses together and look to the heavens to give thanks.

CHAPTER 15

AFTER THREE GLORIOUS WEEKS of sightseeing and leisurely car rides, Gino and I have made plans to spend today on our own. Gino is going to visit distant relatives and childhood friends he has kept in touch with over the years, and I tell him to go and have fun. Secretly, I am happy to have the time alone. While every day has been wonderful, I haven't had much time to write and am eager to add to my story.

Having awakened to another sun-kissed day, we are on the balcony enjoying coffee and pastries. It has become our daily routine to start each morning with French-pressed coffee and pastries that Gino runs out early to pick up.

"So, what will you do with your free time today?" Gino asks. He takes a sip of his coffee.

"I'm not sure yet. I was thinking of going for a walk along the water. Maybe I'll do a little shopping or check out the spa."

"That sounds like a great day. I want you to enjoy yourself. I can't wait to hear all about it when I get back tonight. I should be back by eight at the latest. I will give you a call before I leave. What would you think about dinner and dancing tonight?"

"Now I have a reason to go to the spa and get my hair done! Yes, yes, dancing sounds wonderful!" I get up to clear my plate and feel light on my feet.

Gino takes one more sip of coffee, then stands up and grabs his sport coat. He pulls me in and gives me a long, passionate kiss. After all these years of marriage, his kiss and warm embrace still make me swoon as if each time is the first.

"Dancing it is. See you tonight, Fran. I love you."

As he walks out the door, I go back out on the balcony and smile at the thought of having an entire day to myself. I love spending time with Gino, but it is nice to have a few moments to myself. It will be time to think about what we came here for and what we still need to find. And there's my journal rewrite, which I have not looked at in a few weeks. I get my laptop, bring it to the balcony, and set up a workstation on the bistro table. Then I get another cup of coffee from the French press and settle in. I'm excited to have this time to write. Now that I am finally here, the memories are more clear and vivid. I feel inspired, reinvigorated. The ideas come easily, and I write until lunchtime. Before closing my laptop, I go to the balcony and take a moment to watch the view. This place is heaven on earth. I have had that thought repeatedly over the last few weeks, but if there is one place I would choose to go to feel inspired, this is it.

My stomach rumbles, and I remember that I should grab something to eat. I decide to stop in the hotel lobby on my way to lunch and make a hair appointment at the spa. I want to get my hair done in a chic Italian style, and this is the perfect day to do it. I can surprise Gino when he gets back tonight.

I venture to the hotel lobby, which is so grand it could easily be mistaken for an art gallery. When I stop at the desk to inquire about making a spa appointment, I panic as I wonder whether the staff speaks English. Gino has been doing most of the talking on this trip since Italian is his native tongue. To my relief, they speak fluent English and I do not have to attempt to mime the act of cutting hair. With the appointment scheduled, I browse around the lobby for a few more minutes taking in the artwork on display, the stunning décor, and the view of the water from the veranda.

Finally I make my way out to the café down the street and choose a table outdoors. I order a pizza margherita and a nice glass of wine. For a moment I wish I had my laptop, but I quickly appreciate this opportunity to experience the area with no distractions. I submerge myself in the world around me and pretend that I am one of the many characters charting my way through this magnificent quest to live in the moment. For an hour and a half, I entertain myself with a combination of people-watching and being mesmerized by the hypnotic sights of the waves crashing against the rocks. I feel proud of the accomplishment of simply enjoying my surroundings. Finally the muffled sound of my phone's ringtone pulls me out of my trance, and I fish my mobile out of my purse. When I see the call is from Jane, I answer quickly.

"Hi, Jane!"

"Hi, Fran! How's your trip?"

"Oh, it's wonderful! It has been a dream come true. I have so much to tell you."

Jane asks a few questions, eager to hear every detail about the trip. But I can also hear a difference in her voice, one of pure happiness and exhaustion.

"How about you?" I ask. "Where are you?"

"Well, that's why I'm calling. I have two things to tell you. First, you and Gino are now the proud godparents of Chelsea Marie. She was born last night at eleven fifty-seven our time."

"Oh, Jane! I wish I could be there with you. Congratulations!"

"She's adorable, and I am so in love with her. We are still at the hospital. I can't wait for you to meet her. We are going to have the christening after you both get home."

"I can't wait to meet her. With all my heart, I'm so happy for you and Charlie."

"That's not all. I wanted to call you yesterday to tell you the other news, but obviously I got sidetracked. I heard back about your manuscript. It was a hit. They said it was refreshing and truthful and would be perfect for their new imprint. They can't wait to see the ending."

Sitting at the outdoor café listening to Jane, I am so stunned by this news that it takes me a moment to respond.

"Fran? Fran? Are you still there?"

I'm forming the words with my mouth, but no sound is emerging. Finally, I hear myself say, "Yes, yes, I'm still here."

"Thought I lost you for a moment there. This is such fantastic news. So what do you think?"

"I'm speechless. I just needed a second to process what you said. They really liked it? I can't believe it. They really want to publish it?"

"They want to offer you a contract. I can't tell you what's included because I don't know. But I wanted to tell you the news. I'm so proud of you, Fran. I told you that you never know what can happen."

"You did. I'm so glad I listened to you. Thank you so much for encouraging me to do it. I'm still stunned. I don't think it will sink in for a while."

"This year is shaping up for you, Fran. This is happening; you'd better believe it!"

"I'm so giddy with excitement I can't concentrate on anything else. Before I let you go, how's Luigi? I miss him so much."

"Oh, he's fine. He's such a sweetheart. You will have a hard time pulling him away from the kids. They treat him like he's their baby brother and dress him up. It's hilarious. I think he's happy when he gets his alone time."

"We are so lucky to have you guys. Thank you again for keeping him. I know he enjoys it, but I sure do miss him."

"It's been great. We all love him. Listen, I want to talk more, but I am so tired. I will let you know as soon as I hear anything more about the book. It may not be until you get back. You and Gino have a great time. You have a lot of celebrating to do. I miss you two so much."

"Okay, rest and enjoy your new bundle. I can't wait to meet her and see you all. I miss you, too!"

As I hang up the phone, I am still in shock. I cannot believe the news. Is this happening? Am I going to have a published piece of work? I imagine myself excitedly telling Gino the news.

I look at my watch and see it is almost time for my hair appointment. I head back to the hotel, smiling from ear to ear. I cannot believe it. Maybe this is what I am meant to do. Maybe all this frustration and feeling unfulfilled over the past year has led me here, to this moment. Maybe writing is my calling.

While I'm at the sink, touching up my makeup, I realize that it has been weeks, maybe even months, since I last had self-deprecating thoughts or feelings of hopelessness. I have been truly happy, enjoying myself so fully that I haven't even given much thought to my previous reality. Whatever the case, I now have another reason to feel happy: I have something new to work toward. I will be someone I can feel proud of—not because of my journal rewrite, but because I fought through my despair and didn't succumb. While I know this is just the beginning and I am sure to have more tribulations ahead, at least for the moment, I have a goal—and I know I owe it all to Jane. It would never have occurred to me to even investigate the publishing idea had it not been for her.

As I enter the salon, I am immediately welcomed by a lovely receptionist with a big, beautiful smile emphasized by fire-engine-red lipstick. Her chin-length black hair angles toward her face perfectly, every single strand in place. She hands me a crystal flute of champagne, greets me by name in an Italian accent, and asks me to follow her into the lounge. Sparkling chandeliers hang from the ceiling, and mirrors line the walls. The plush, velvety plum-colored chairs exude elegance and glamour. She invites me to have a seat and says my stylist will be along soon. Thanking her, I sit in one of the chairs, thinking this place is beyond nice. Just when I think it cannot get any better, it does.

"*Buongiorno*, Francesca!" There is so much excitement in her voice; anyone listening would think we are best friends. I look up and see a beautiful woman walking toward me. At the sight of her, I feel myself shrinking into the couch. *Silly*, I think—*you have just as much to offer.* I stand up proud and tall as the woman comes to greet me.

"I'm Katerina," she says, and she links arms with me and guides me to her styling station. "Now, Francesca, what shall we do with your hair today?"

We talk for a few minutes about what look I want to achieve. Katerina nods in excitement at the drastic changes she is going to create. Her demeanor, clothing style, and hair are exactly what I want to replicate: sophistication and elegance all wrapped up in one. I can tell she understands what I want. I take a deep breath, anticipating what is to come, and then I sit back, exhale, and relax.

Thinking about the phone call from Jane and looking around at my surroundings filled with marble, gold, and champagne, I cannot believe where my life has recently taken me. I feel like I am living in someone else's world. The old me would have questioned if she were worthy enough to experience this, but the new me is ignoring such thoughts and looking forward. I take another sip of the complimentary champagne and feel its calming effects. As I feel Katerina getting to work on the unruly mess on my head, I drift into a meditative state.

I cannot remember the last time I had my hair trimmed, let alone styled. It feels great to be in the hands of a master of her craft, not worrying about the outcome as I usually would. I have complete faith in her skill and ability to make me the best version of myself. This time, I am completely relinquishing any hold I habitually have on myself. I am finally taking control of my feelings to generate a more optimistic outcome. Gone are the days of disparaging remarks that seem to creep into my mind so easily without being invited. I am learning to welcome unfamiliar territory with whatever positive force I can muster from deep within.

As Katerina finishes making the last few touches on my hair, she asks if I am ready to see it. As if unveiling a work of art, she slowly spins my chair around so I can view the finished masterpiece. I look at the mirror, and it seems as if someone else's reflection is looking back at me. Slowly I process the changes. My normally mousy-brown hair is now blond with some dark brown lowlights. Katerina has brought the length up from just below the shoulder to a chic chin-length bob. Even my blue eyes look brighter. I look and feel more alive than I have in years. A tear comes to my eye. I have no idea why and quickly wipe it away before Katerina sees it.

"It's beautiful! I love it. It's exactly the look I was going for." Stunned, I keep looking in the mirror and smiling uncontrollably. I thank Katerina over and over.

A drastic change was definitely past due. I was prepared for the alteration but unprepared for the emotions it is evoking. I feel transformed not only on the outside but on the inside. I used to get my hair done more frequently, but over the years I slowly stopped because it seemed so expensive. It was not that I couldn't afford it; it was more like I didn't want to. This entire experience, however, is making me reconsider. If getting my hair done can make me feel good about myself, maybe I should reconsider its value and do it more often. The lift in my mood is having a huge impact on me today. It has inspired me to continue with my transformation. Gino is in for a big surprise.

Alive, excited, energized, and feeling beautiful for the first time I can remember in quite some time, I head out the salon door with my head held high on a mission for a beautiful dress to wear tonight. I packed several dresses for this trip, but I want something different, something that will show how I am feeling right now. Something Italian.

I browse through several clothing boutiques until my eyes are drawn to the perfect dress. It is a gorgeous blush color with spaghetti straps that crisscross into a low-cut back. It has a narrow gold band belt that fits snugly around the waist and enough loose material to flare around my knees. I am not usually the type to meander, shopping the day away. I suppose that is why I am having so much fun today—that and I am feeling so good and cannot wait to share my excitement with Gino.

In the next shop window I come to, I see a gorgeous pair of heels—gold, with an open toe—and they are calling to me. I walk into the fancy boutique, and immediately a saleswoman comes over to talk with me. Recognizing that I am not skilled in Italian, she transitions to English beautifully and without hesitation. I point out the shoes I am interested in, and she brings me a pair in my size to try on. They have a three-inch heel and a sparkle on the ankle strap, enough to be fun without looking overly fancy. At the register, the store owner shows me a gold clutch that complements the shoes so perfectly I decide to get it. It is the perfect ensemble for tonight, and it will go nicely with my cream silk wrap when it gets cool in the evening.

As I leave the boutique, I hear my phone buzz coming from my purse. Juggling my shopping bags, I find the phone in the black abyss and pull it out.

"Hey, babe. I wanted to let you know I'm on my way. I should be there in a couple of hours. I'm looking forward to our date."

"I'll be ready. Drive carefully, and I will see you when you get here. I love you."

"I love you, too. See you soon." With my purchases in tow, I walk at a leisurely pace back to the hotel.

Eagerly awaiting Gino's return, I take a long, luxurious bubble bath, careful not to mess up my hair. I have not treated myself to a bubble bath in years. Then I put on my new dress and shoes. I look in the mirror and admired my new haircut and lowlights. I am happy with how it turned out and how good it makes me feel. I know our time here is slowly winding down. I want this evening to be extra special. I feel it, and I think Gino does too.

I put on the finishing touches—my lipstick and favorite diamond stud earrings—and I walk out onto the balcony to wait. Not moments later, I hear the door to the room click open. It is exactly eight o'clock, just as he promised. As he walks up behind me, I turn toward him, and he stops dead in his tracks. I have never seen him look at me the way he is looking at me right now. It is a look of surprise, shock, longing, and marvel. Although he has not yet said anything, his expression gives me a feeling of complete delight. I feel like the most beautiful person in the world.

"Fran, you . . . you just took my breath away."

At a loss for any more words, Gino walks up to me. This moment between us is silent, yet I see his emotions in the crinkles around his eyes as he smiles and the sweet gestures of his hands as they frame my face. Finally he finds his voice again.

"I almost didn't recognize you when you had your back to me. You look absolutely beautiful, but you always do to me. I hope you know that and never forget it. I can't believe you cut your hair. I love it. Do you like it?"

"Yes, I do. I was a little surprised at first. It took me a minute to recognize myself, but I love it. It was time for a change, and I felt energized in a way I hadn't felt in a while. Isn't it funny how getting your haircut can do that? So, after that, I decided to go shopping. I got this dress and these shoes." Smiling, I strike a pose to show off the new ensemble.

"You look gorgeous. And I'm so glad to hear you had a great day. Listen, give me five minutes. I want to jump in the shower before we go. I want to look respectable escorting my wife out tonight." He winks at me and gives me a kiss on the cheek before going back inside.

I turn back to look out over the balcony. My heart is full of peace. I feel as if my heart is actually overflowing with the amount of love I hold for my husband. I watch the boats and ships below as they bob and sway to the gentle music of the water lapping against the rocks. My eyes are drawn to the line where the sea meets the sky, where the setting sun blends with the pastel blues and pinks. Breathing in the fresh sea air, I think about how far I have come over the last year. I think about where we are going and the changes we need to make. I think about life, and the true inspiration of the natural beauty in this world and how happy it makes me feel. And, for the first time, I think about the novel of my life. I have not called my journal rewrite anything other than that, a rewrite. But if I am truly doing this and putting it in print, it is a story of my life. Perhaps it will be the first of many, but, for now, I will settle for the one. Writing has gotten me through this past year; it has been a therapeutic respite to save me from the burdens of my unbridled thoughts. I have been a prisoner of my mind for far too long. Such a prison is hard to escape and hard for others to understand. But I feel as if I can finally let the reins go—or at least relax my grip on them.

I remain lost in my thoughts, as I often am, until Gino comes up behind me and slides his arms around my waist. After I gather my wrap and clutch, we head to the hotel lobby and walk out to join the lively scene on the streets. Even though it is a weekday, the streets are filled with couples and groups of people heading toward their nightly ritual of gathering with friends to enjoy another beautiful evening. There is a reason to celebrate the end of every day, and it is contagious.

I ask Gino where we should go for dinner. "I didn't even think about making reservations anywhere. With all these people, do you think we will find something?"

"I already have that covered." Gino puts his left hand on the small of my back and guides me to a little restaurant filled with lights and laughter. The place is so packed, it is hard to believe any more people can fit through the door. We follow the man holding menus and miraculously wend our way through the crowded bar and the maze of tables. I can hear a band playing a piece that sounds like Henry Mancini's "Moon River," and as I glance over my right shoulder, I get a brief glimpse of the dance floor. It is a small sea of women in colorful dresses and sparkling jewelry and men looking elegantly handsome in their suits. I feel I have been transported to another era, when dancing, eating, laughing, and drinking were enough to fill the soul.

The man with the menus seats us in an alcove surrounded by large plants and strung around with miniature lights. It is a little hideaway amid all the people. As I look around, I see several alcoves of different sizes. Some are large enough to seat ten or more, and others, like this one, are intimate spaces for two to four. Sliding into the booth, I am amazed at how quieter it is in this little niche compared to being out in the main part of the restaurant. The din of voices is softened. I can still hear the music faintly.

"Gino, how have we never been here before? It's wonderful. I feel like I'm on a movie set waiting for Cary Grant to walk through the door."

Laughing, Gino takes my hand. "I thought you would like it here. An old friend of mine suggested it. He didn't let us down. It is nice."

A waiter appears to give us each a glass of champagne, then disappears.

Gino says, "I hope you don't mind. I went ahead and ordered our meal in courses so we can enjoy the evening and dance away." He holds up his glass and says, "To my beautiful wife—for all the years behind us and all those still to come. I love you."

I pick up my glass and clink it with his, then take a sip. It is pink champagne, I marvel. As I set my glass down, Gino slides out from the booth, extends a hand to me, and says, "May I have this dance?"

My husband is always a perfect gentleman, but tonight his gentlemanly courtesies are on full display. It is as if we are the leading man and lady in a romantic movie. We dance and dine, enjoying each other's company. It is an evening to add to our collection of life moments worth remembering, and I am determined to remember every detail.

AT THE START OF our fourth week here, we are sitting on the balcony having breakfast. This morning, instead of running out to the café for pastries and coffee, Gino has called for room service—and it is a feast. Eggs, French toast, fruit, yogurt, orange juice, and pastries—just the sight of it spread on the table is enough to make a person gain five pounds. There have been so many fantastic details about this trip, but one thing is for sure: the food is fabulous, and we have eaten well. Fortunately, we have walked a lot, too.

"I hear it's going to get hot today," Gino says between sips of coffee. "What do you think about heading to Camogli and going to our secret beach? It's a great day for the water."

"I would love that. I'll go change and get my things together. I'll be ready in twenty."

As long as we have been here, we haven't yet gone to the beach. We have only admired it from the balcony and the car. Excited for a day on the water, I grab a pen and paper to put in my bag so I can make some notes to add to my book. I still have not told Gino my news. This will be the perfect time to tell him without any distractions. Plus, as our trip winds down, I am increasingly thinking about home and what it will be like when we return. I know Gino must get back to the shop—and I miss Luigi, and of course, I want to see Jane's new baby girl. But what's next? Gino and I have talked about making changes, but only in general terms. I know he is open to change, but I am afraid that if we go home with no ideas, decisions, or plans, we will settle back into our old situation. While this trip has been a blessing in more ways than I can count, I'm not sure it will be enough to sustain me indefinitely. *If only we could live here forever*, I think—we could live in paradise and let all our worries disappear.

About forty-five minutes later, our beach gear is in the car, and Gino and I are out on the road heading to a beautiful, secluded beach near Camogli. We call it our secret beach because only the locals know how to get to it, and it is rarely occupied. From the road, one sees only rocks and water. But if you know where to walk, you can skirt the rocks and find a perfect sandy beach. It is one of the few beaches in the area that captures the charm of the land.

The day is perfect. The bright blue sky is dotted with high, puffy clouds in magnificent shapes. It is the kind of sky that makes you feel as if you are floating if you stare at it. The last time we were here, we both fell asleep and woke up sunburnt. This time, fortunately, we have a large umbrella to provide shade.

We are lying next to each other on a blanket. Gino's nose is buried in a book. I turn onto my right side to face him. "Gino, I have something exciting to tell you."

He marks his place in the book and closes it, then turns toward me and takes my hand. He is looking at me intently, encouraging me to tell him without saying a word.

"Do you know all those notes I'm always jotting down?" Gino nods. "Well, last year, when I was going through that grim time, I was looking for something on my computer, and I found my old journal from my trip to Italy the year we met. I started reading it, and gradually I found myself turning it into a story. It wasn't anything big. I'm not sure how I got started on it; I never even liked writing assignments in school. But the more I wrote, the better I started feeling. It became a form of therapy for me. It gave me purpose and a temporary sense of fulfillment."

"I can understand that," Gino says. "Why didn't you ever tell me this before?"

"I guess because of how I felt at the time. I felt like I had nothing to give or offer anyone. When I say that out loud, it sounds funny. I am grateful for everything I have, but I'm not happy with myself. I haven't been for a long time. After I lost my job, I had no path. I wanted to find something that is a career and not just a job, but I was too afraid to venture out of my comfort zone. I kept looking for ways to change my thoughts, opinions, actions—anything that might guide me somewhere, anywhere, but I didn't know what to do. And most of my old social network was gone. I have always believed that problems work out eventually, but when they didn't, I led myself into this black hole of despair. I felt so lost. People have their struggles to deal with, you know? It's easy for onlookers to make suggestions, but unless they have been in the same situation, they can't understand the extreme pain that comes from this struggle I've been fighting. And, Gino, I can only burden you with so much. After a while, it gets old. Besides, I can only take so much of it myself."

I shift my position and sit up, and Gino does too.

"But that's not what I wanted to tell you. That's the backdrop. Anyway, so I have been writing regularly, and I've done almost a hundred pages. One day I was on the phone with Jane, and she asked me to send her a copy. It took a lot of encouragement, but eventually I did, and she showed it to someone at her publishing company. And, well, they loved it. They might want to publish it as a novel."

As I'm telling Gino this, his eyes get big. "It's getting published? Fran, that is amazing!"

"It *might* be," I said. "They want to see the ending first. But Jane says they like it."

"I'm so proud of you, Fran. I can't believe you didn't tell me earlier."

"I know, I know. I wanted to, but . . . as I told Jane, writing helped me through a tough time. I never intended for it to be published. If I didn't show it to anyone, it was still mine. It took a lot of encouragement from Jane before I was ready to let her see it. If the publisher hadn't liked it, I'm not sure how I would have taken the news. But this might be what I have been searching for. I finally feel like I have a direction and a purpose, something beyond showing up for a job that doesn't mean anything to me. I know you understand that because of your passion for your shop."

"I do."

"But I also know my friends and family. I don't think they see things that way. I think they would say, 'Work is work; that's just how life is.' I can't accept that way of thinking. If I'm going to live my life, I want to live. Maybe writing is what I'm meant to do. But here's the thing. We came on this trip to find answers for both of us, and we haven't discussed our plans for after we get home. I have an idea that has been slowly rolling around in my head. I wanted to run it by you to get your thoughts."

"I know, Fran. I have been thinking a lot about that, too. Before you say anything, I want you to know what a wonderful woman you are and how happy you make me. I want you to be happy. I told you from the start that we would get through this together, and we will. We have come a long way to find answers, and I am open to ideas and willing to do whatever we need to do to make us happy forever."

Gino smiles and kisses me. He takes my hand again as we sit under the umbrella, listening to the sound of the waves.

"So here is what I have been thinking about. I love spending time with you at the shop. I love helping with the displays, handling the register, and being with you while you work. You have done a phenomenal job with the shop, and I'm only sorry that it has taken me so long to see it. I know the local market is more interested in furniture than boats. It's not something we have ever discussed—at least not in the last ten years—but what if we move? What if we go up north along the shore? Maybe New England? I know it would be hard to build the business back, but wouldn't it be great if you could build the boats you have always dreamed of? We could buy a shop near the water and live close by so that you wouldn't have a long commute. We could cut the hours. We could work the shop together and I could continue to write. We would both be doing something we love. Neither of us is satisfied with what we have been doing. Why not make it better and change the things that are plaguing us? And who knows—a fresh start might open us up to new ideas."

I can tell Gino is processing everything I have said. I start thinking about everything we would need to do: sell the shop, sell the house, buy a shop, buy a new house—and find new customers. It would not be such an easy feat, but it wouldn't be impossible. Gino had turned an old, dilapidated barn into a woodworking haven and one of the most successful shops. Imagine what we could do together. I am excited thinking of all the possibilities. I silently cross my fingers, hoping Gino will be excited too.

We sit for a long time, not saying anything—probably no more than thirty minutes, but it feels like hours. The heat is getting to me—today is the hottest day since we arrived—and I can feel the sweat running down my face. I am beside myself, wondering what Gino is thinking, but rather than add more to the heavy discussion, I jump up to take a dip in the water. We are the only ones on the beach. I feel my toes sinking into the sand as the water rushes up and retreats into the ocean. I can feel my breath keeping cadence with the waves. As I inhale, the water rushes in. As I exhale, trying to blow out the unnecessary chatter in my mind, the water rushes back out. The cycle could almost put me into a hypnotized state, but I keep thinking if there was a better way to have presented my idea. But to my surprise, Gino walks up beside me and takes my hand. I turn to look at him. He is looking straight to sea with an expression I have not seen before. It is one of surprise, excitement, and concern all at the same time.

"You are probably wondering what I am thinking."

I can't speak. Just as my thoughts are about to run away with me, Gino continues.

"I love the idea. I know things can't stay the way they have been. It will take a lot of work; we will have to put everything we have into a new shop. But I love your passion. As much as I didn't want to admit it, I was slowly becoming distant from the shop anyway. You are right. My dream has always been to build boats, and while I love making furniture, it isn't my dream. We had a life there, and the shop was doing well. Why mess with it? I can see now that the safe answer isn't always the best. I think the shop has run its course. It's time to move on. Let's go for it. Let's see where it takes us. If we are in it together, I'm happy to be anywhere with you, Fran."

Still looking out to sea, Gino squeezes my hand. I know this is a big decision, but it feels right for us. The immense relief I feel is like setting down a heavy load and finding that it was even larger than I knew. I have been carrying a burden for both of us. Finally my journey is at an end. I asked the universe a question and finally received an answer. My path of self-discovery has led both of us to a new adventure.

We spend the rest of the day finding solace in the water and sun. It is as if we have visible wounds, and the earth and sky are medicinal forces in our healing process. Knowing how long I have struggled to find my path in life, I am surprised when I realize Gino, as strong and secure as he is, has also been searching for his. I think we both feel complete relief and utter satisfaction in knowing that we came here to Italy for one purpose, and we have accomplished it. While it has been soul-searching and hard for us, the result has put us on the same trajectory, and for that I am thankful.

The path ahead will be a challenge, but we are both up to tackling it. There will be pressure but a good kind of pressure and necessary. The possibilities are limitless, and my mind is in constant overdrive now that we have had this much-needed discussion. I am truly excited about what's going to be in our future.

CHAPTER 17

WHEN WE ARRIVED IN Italy, it felt like we had all the time in the world. This past month has flown by. Part of me wishes I could stay here forever, but I know reality eventually comes into play. I cannot continue living in a world of make-believe, no matter how temporary. I can, however, make my new reality my dream. All the discussions Gino and I have had, both before and during this trip, have opened our eyes to how we see and understand each other. Knowing that we have so much change ahead of us is exciting, and sharing this journey is even more thrilling to me than I imagined. Although we have big plans, it's nice to know we are not in a rush. The sooner, the better, but fortunately, we have time on our side.

We are making our final preparations for our return stateside. We have a few more days to spend in our beloved town where it all began.

Gino comes onto the balcony, his morning coffee in hand, and sits next to me. "Babe, is there anything special you want to do today?"

I stretch my arms above my head and prop my legs on the balcony railing. "I just want to enjoy the day. No big plans. Just be."

I am still in my nightgown. For a moment I imagine a fairy-tale world in which time will stand still if I don't get dressed, and we won't have to make any preparations to leave. Yet I am excited to leave, too. As we talk, I admire the view. There is so much I want to do to start our new adventure. Soon I am just staring up at the beautiful, untouched sky. Most people call it daydreaming, but that word doesn't capture it. My brain is abuzz with activity, processing ideas at warp speed.

Gino goes to the balcony and looks across the water. "I can't believe we have a few more days of this. It's been great. I can't believe how much I've changed in the last few weeks—and for me to take notice is something! I feel good. Like I've shed some unwanted baggage on my shoulders that I didn't know I had."

"I was just thinking about how much I love it here," I reply. I love the way I feel being here. I love the way we start our mornings together on this balcony. The sea, the beautiful boats on the water . . . I'm going to miss it."

"It is pretty spectacular. Maybe it's time to create new rituals at home in our new place. If we do what we're planning, we will have a lot more time together. Maybe once we get everything situated, we can make it a goal to come back here more often. Or we can even think about visiting new places. We haven't done much vacationing over the last several years. I think it's time we make that a priority."

"That sounds like a great idea," I say as I get up and join Gino by the balcony railing. "Hey, how about the pool today? While we're there, we can research some options. I've already sent an email to a realtor up in Massachusetts that Jane recommended a long time ago. We could look for something along the Cape. I don't know if she's still active, but if she isn't, maybe she can suggest someone. It's a start."

I hug Gino and stay nestled in the warmth and comfort of his arms. Breathing in the fresh ocean air, feeling the sun slowly cast its warmth on me as it gets higher in the beautiful blue sky, I capture this moment in my mind, not wanting to forget anything. I think of all the joy this trip has brought us and how much I want this moment to last.

Lounging by the pool was a fantastic idea. The décor, reminiscent of the 1950s, makes me feel like a movie star. Beautiful blue-and-white-striped awnings with long white fringe span the doors between the pool and the hotel lobby. Matching umbrellas with impeccably clean, shiny white tables flank the opposite side of the entrance to the pool, with the shimmering pool reflections caught in the middle. The views of the ocean lie beyond. The sounds of the ocean are barely audible, but the smell of the saltwater is powerful, letting you know how close you are to the water. Normally Gino is so involved in a book that he is oblivious to his surroundings, but now that he has had some time to let things sink in over the last few days, he is in full preparation mode. It is exciting to see his old enthusiasm again—to see that spark, burned out for so long, finally reignited. My initial worry that we might not find what we came here for has been replaced with inspiration and joy. Ideas flow out of both of us, and the anticipation of it all is anything but overwhelming.

In the middle of our planning, I realize I had better let Jane know we will be back soon. "Gino," I say, "I'm going to call Jane to let her know we'll pick Luigi up on Saturday. I'm so excited to see her and the baby. She will be thrilled at our news, too—except that we are moving."

"I have a few ideas for where to put the shop," Gino says. "It might be cheaper to go a little inland, but as long as we are near the coast, I think it will work." I know he did not hear a word I said.

Excited, I call Jane. "Good morning! Oh, wait, sorry. I forgot about the time difference."

"Fran! I'm so happy to hear from you. No, no, it's fine. This is a good time anyway. Chelsea is sleeping. So, did you tell Gino? What did he say? When are you coming home?"

"Oh, Jane, it's so good to hear your voice. I miss you all so much. Yes, I did tell Gino, and he's happy for me. I have so much to tell you. First, we are coming home in a few days. We're landing around two on Saturday, so we should be home around six, I think."

"Oh my gosh. That's great. I can't wait to see you! I figured you would be coming back sometime soon. So, did you accomplish everything you wanted to do on the trip?"

"Yes. It's been good; I'm glad we did this. And that leads to something else I have to tell you. We've decided we're moving, and we're excited about it."

"What? Where? When?" Jane sounds surprised, but I can tell she is happy for us.

"Well, as soon as we find something. Gino is going to open a new shop on the coast. We don't have a place yet, but we will start looking right away. We are thinking New England. No more long commutes. No more long days. We will do it together, and I'll keep writing on the side. Jane, I'm so excited.

I haven't had something to be proud of or look forward to in a long time. This is it. We are finally doing something."

"I am so happy for you both. I know you have been dealing with unhappiness for a while now. I'm just so glad you both have found your answer. I will miss you when you move. But I am truly happy for you both. Oh, you should contact that realtor I told you about a long time ago. Remember? I forget her name."

"I have. I sent her an email already to see if she can help us."

"That's fantastic. I can't believe it. I'm just so excited for you guys."

"Thanks, Jane. Listen, I don't want to keep you long. I just wanted to give you the news. I can't wait to see you all this weekend. Tell everyone we said hello, and we will see you soon."

"You guys have safe travels. See you Saturday."

It feels good to tell someone about our plan. I have so much to do to make it happen, yet I feel right. Sitting back in my lounge chair, knowing Gino is happy too, I close my eyes and listen to the voices of people talking and swimming around me and let my mind drift. The feel of the sun warming my body, the occasional droplets of water from people splashing in the pool, the voices, the scent of sunscreen lingering in the air— my senses are so filled that I know I am alive and well at this moment. I feel good.

A day at the pool was just what we needed: time to collect our thoughts and ideas and pull together some of the information we want to research. By the evening, my mind is reeling at all the possibilities, and my sun-drenched body is exhausted. It is exhilarating to know we are on the cusp of something life-changing. By the time I make it to the bed,

Gino has already drifted off, and I am asleep almost before my head can hit the pillow.

The following morning, I wake up to a note on the pillow beside me. I squint at the clock through sleepy eyes. It's not quite seven. Maybe Gino went out early to grab our breakfast. I reach for the note and read it.

Good morning, sweetheart. You were sleeping so soundly I didn't have the heart to wake you. I wanted to get an early start on making some new connections about the shop before we leave. I'll text you later when I'm on my way back. I will be back this afternoon. I love you.

Gino

I roll onto my back and stare at the ceiling. I am a little excited to have the morning to myself. I have been eager to finish my manuscript, and I am even more so now that our days are dwindling. I want to complete it before we leave. I have so much I want to say, and I need to get it out now before it has a chance to fade from my mind. At least if I get the ideas down, I can edit them when we get home.

I quickly get out of bed. At first I think about writing out on the balcony, but I feel inspired and decide the pool would be the perfect place to write. I put on my bathing suit and my light blue paisley-print dress to cover up. I assemble my sandals, hat, and pool bag. It is still incredibly early, so hardly anyone should be there. It will be the perfect scene to gaze at as I gather all the ideas in my head, eagerly waiting to spill onto the computer screen.

As I walk out onto the pool deck, I am relieved to see I am the only one present. I don't always prefer to be alone, but there is something uniquely refreshing about morning solitude. It gives me some undisturbed time to enjoy a beautiful morning and plan my events for the day. I stand beside the sparkling pool water with my bag on my shoulder. I look around, surrounded by impenetrable stillness, listening to the sounds of the ocean before voices drown it out, taking in the smell of the saltwater before it is replaced by the strong smells of breakfast and sunscreen. It is another instance of many to add to my collection of moments too good to be passed by and not noticed.

I make my way over to the umbrella table at the far corner of the pool and set up my workstation. I am in a perfect spot. Still visible are the ocean to my right and the bright striped awnings hovering over the pool entrance across the way to my left. I am close enough to the entrance to see when other guests arrive but far from the commotion of people coming and going. I am distant enough from the pool's edge that I will not have to worry about getting water on my computer, and my umbrella is perfectly aligned so that I will have constant shade all day. It is the most enviable spot on the pool deck, and I am glad to have secured it.

I feel inspired, emboldened, and energized. I am going to miss Portofino. I will miss the feelings, memories, experiences, and mostly the power this place has had over me all these weeks. It has been my muse and outlet, helping me find a creative balance that I never knew existed within me. Here, I found the stimulus to continue writing. And here I learned I hold more power in my heart and mind than I ever thought possible.

As I sit in front of my computer, my face mirrored on the blank screen, I imagine all the things I have experienced and witnessed in my lifetime. I think about the moments that make up my life and have made that life worth living. Everything I've seen, everyone I've known, has impacted me in some way, some more than others, but none more than Gino. He has always inspired me and believed in me. He has been my lifeline. I think that is why this writing adventure I have been on has meant so much to me. I have finally put into words the impact his life has made on mine. I hope that he knows how much better my life is because of him.

I am engrossed in my work, my fingers tapping along the keyboard in what has become a familiar pulse. I am so oblivious that it takes me a second to recognize a looming presence above my computer screen. Looking up, I see Antonio, one of the many restaurant employees we have slowly become friends with over our weeks here. He is a nice young man with long blond hair tied back in a ponytail at the nape of his neck and wearing a tuxedo, the customary uniform for most of the restaurant staff.

"*Buon giorno*, Ms. Francesca!" he bellows out. He has a lot of energy for so early in the morning. "Would you care to have your breakfast out here? I am more than happy to bring you something."

"*Buon giorno*, Antonio. *Si*, that would be lovely. Perhaps coffee and a chocolate croissant?"

"Prego, prego. I will bring it right out." He vanishes back into the hotel before I can thank him.

Happy to take a break, I look at the bottom of the computer screen to catch a glimpse of the time. I have been so good about not letting time rule me here. Gino and I have been at the mercy of only the day and the night. Still, I am curious to know how long I have been out here. It was seven-thirty when I slid into my chair. It is now just after nine. I know the quiet will not last much longer. I am proud of how much I have managed to type out in the last hour and a half. If I continue at the rate I have been working the last few days, I should wrap this up soon.

Antonio returns with a tray and sets it down. "Ms. Francesca, here you are. *Prego, prego*, enjoy." On the tray are a pot of coffee, a mini pitcher of cream, a sugar bowl, and a matching cup and saucer. On another plate is the chocolate croissant, which I cannot wait to sink my teeth into.

As Antonio bows and backs away, I smile and say, "*Grazie, grazie.*"

While I am enjoying breakfast, my phone lights up and buzzes. Gino is calling.

"Good morning!" I say, smiling and making myself comfortable in the chair.

"Good morning to you, too. I'm sorry I didn't say goodbye before I left. It was so early. I didn't want to wake you."

"That's okay. Where are you?"

"Up the coast about an hour and a half away. I woke up early and couldn't get back to sleep. I was thinking about where I will get the accessories I need for the boat parts. I can't get them state-side and I want to know what the parts are like before I order them. I got to thinking that I should have a few backups. Since we are leaving soon and it's easier to do in person, I thought I would drive to a couple of places and meet people. I'm so glad I decided to do it, too. Now that I know them and they know me, it will be easier to do business over the phone."

"That was smart thinking."

"Besides, I knew you wanted to get some writing done."

"You know me all too well! I did, and I have." As we talk, I walk to the side of the pool, where the water, as smooth as a mirror, begs me to dip my toes in.

"I figured you would welcome the time. And the sooner I left, the earlier I could be back."

"Yeah. I have gotten a lot done already. I came to the pool early to write. I'm still the only one here. I love it; it's so peaceful. Antonio even brought me breakfast. It's like a little sanctuary, but I do miss you."

"I wish I were there with you, too. How about dinner instead?"

"Definitely. But don't rush—whenever you get back this afternoon is fine. I'd like to finish the book before we leave."

"Okay. I'll let you get back to work. I'll text you when I'm on my way. I love you."

"I love you, too."

I slide my feet into my sandals and walk around the pool a couple of times to stretch my legs. Knowing I am fully committed now, I am not breaking camp. I am on a roll and will ride it out as long as I can. Admiring everything in my path as I return to my table, I sit, pour another cup of coffee, and continue writing.

Lately, once I commit myself to a task, I get so involved that I am completely unaware of the world around me, and today has been no exception. I have been working steadily since I got off the phone with Gino, and I have not looked up once. Once the ideas start flowing, I am afraid to take a break for fear they will not come back. I am so absorbed in my work that I did not even notice my breakfast tray has been taken away and replaced with a pitcher of water and lemons, or every chair and table at the pool is now occupied, or the sounds of the band that plays on weekday afternoons, nor the pool water that has been soaking my bag for the last several hours because the bag fell off the back of my chair and into the direct path of a miniature river, or that Gino has sent me several text messages and even tried to call me to let me know he is on his way.

I did not notice that Gino pulled up a chair next to me. Finally reaching a point where I am struggling for ideas, I slowly come out of my bubble, and I am stunned to look up and see Gino staring at me with a smile.

"How long have you been sitting there?" I ask.

"Hours," Gino says as he kicks back and props his feet up on the chair next to me. Laughing, he adds, "No, I just got here a few minutes ago. It's nice to see you so deep in thought! No wonder you didn't pick up when I called."

"I know. When I get into a groove, I don't want to stop. It's great. My mind runs so fast. I've never had this feeling before, but I love it. I think it's partly because of the topic, though, too. It's about us and being here, so the writing is easy. But I'm so glad you are here now. I'm done for today—my brain and fingers are worn out. Besides, I have wanted to go for a swim all day. That water looks divine."

"I'll go change. Want to have a poolside dinner? I can stop by the bar and order for us on my way back."

"Yes, that sounds great. I'll do a caprese pizza with a side salad. And how about a bottle of red wine? You pick."

"Sounds good. I'll be back."

As Gino heads upstairs, I close my laptop and slide it into my pool bag. I stretch my arms and feel the release in my shoulders, neck, and back. I feel so good. I am so grateful for the amount of writing I have done today.

The next couple of days fly by. Now that my book is almost done and Gino has taken care of everything he needs to do here for the business, we have been lounging at the pool. Gino is finding his excitement in staying in constant contact with the realtor, which has allowed me to invest the last few hours of this precious time in finishing my pages. It is like a race. I can see the finish line. I am almost there. I want to cross the line, yet I don't want the end to come. It's a funny but good feeling.

As I strike the last key that puts the last character on the page, I feel a sense of release wash through my entire being. The feelings are so indescribable that I am pulled out of my silent reverie. When I open my eyes, I see Gino staring back at me. I do not have to say a word. He knows. And his smile is so bright I feel a few tears spring to my eyes. All my labor over this past year has finally culminated in a finished manuscript. I know I still have the work of rereading and revising ahead, but the draft is done.

"I think this calls for a bottle of champagne," Gino says. "Let's mark this momentous occasion with a toast. For completing your book, our trip, and a new beginning."

CHAPTER 18

Our flight home is happily ordinary but exceptionally long. After such a long time away from home, anticipation has finally caught up with me, and I feel we cannot get home fast enough. This is the longest we had ever left Luigi, and I cannot wait to feel his almost one-hundred-pound body crash into me with excitement. The thought of Luigi's eagerness to be loved and have my undivided attention as he melts onto the floor and rolls over for his much-anticipated belly rub paints a joyful picture in my mind. I have missed him so much.

Luigi was a gift from the one above. Gino and I are dog lovers, but we were always working, so the thought of getting a dog never entered our minds. One day at the bank, one of my customers mentioned the animal shelter was over capacity and dogs were in desperate need of homes. It was a Friday. Gino had come home early that afternoon. I asked him if he wanted to go for a drive, and we ended up at the shelter. I told myself we were only looking around, but the moment my eyes locked on Luigi, it was love at first sight. He was so scared. Seeing him curled up into a tight ball with his cute head resting on his paw melted me. I think Gino had the same reaction, and before we knew it, we were walking out of the shelter with a new addition to our family. It was one of the best spur-of-the-moment decisions we have made over the years.

Thinking about Luigi reminds me of how much I have missed my parents. Normally I pick up the phone and call them often, but I haven't spoken to them since before we left. Suddenly I have the overwhelming urge to see them. I have learned to listen to my feelings, especially when they are strong. *That is one of the first things I need to do when we get home*, I think. I am not putting things off anymore.

I feel the bump of the plane as the wheels hit the tarmac. As we coast the runway, I pray that Luigi hasn't forgotten me. The time it takes to taxi to our gate feels excruciatingly long. Next we wait again while everyone in front of us gathers their bags and files out. I imagine myself tearing through the crowd and sprinting to the baggage claim, but even if that were possible, my manners would get the best of me.

Finally it is our turn to deplane. I can't believe how different everything looks to me. Visiting another country is life-changing—something everyone should experience at least once—but no matter how long you are gone, the feeling of coming home is like no other. It is the comfort of the familiar and the satisfaction of knowing you are in your element.

I call Jane from the road to let her know we are about twenty minutes from home. Jane, knowing we will be tired, has kindly brought Luigi over to our house so that we don't have to pick him up.

At the sight of our house, I am immediately excited, but my excitement turns into sadness for just a few moments when I remember that this will not be our home for much longer. Gino and I have spent so many years together here. It was our first house as a married couple, and soon we will be casting it off like an old shoe. Even when you need new shoes, throwing away that comfortable old pair is still hard. I know the sadness will be only temporary; a house is only a home if you are in it. I change gears and become excited once again that we are home now.

As we pull into our driveway, I see Jane holding baby Chelsea, with Charlie standing proudly next to them while the kids play in the yard with Luigi. Jane and Charlie wave with huge smiles. As we get out of the car, Luigi runs to us and is so excited he is not sure what to do. He jumps, flops on the ground for a belly rub, then jumps again, his tail flapping wildly the entire time. Laughing, Gino and I drop our bags and let Luigi have his way until he seems content. In the meantime, everyone else has made their way to us.

"Jane!" I hug Jane, careful not to bump into the bundle in her arms.

"Fran, Gino, meet Chelsea!" Jane says, moving the baby blanket away from the baby's tiny face. Gino and I peek at the adorable baby girl and smile.

"Oh, she is so beautiful. You all must be so happy. Are you guys getting any sleep?"

"More than I expected. She is actually easy-going."

"Congratulations, Dad," Gino says as he shakes Charlie's hand.

"There's one more surprise we have waiting for you," says Jane.

Charlie opens the front door. Standing there, holding hands and smiling, are my parents. They step outside and start down the path to greet us.

"Mom! Dad! What are you doing here?" I race to them and throw my arms around them. Something is different about them. My mom, who normally dresses for comfort, is wearing a beautiful powder-blue summer dress with a deep V-neck and cap sleeves with slight ruffles. Her sandals are fancy as well. I have always thought she is beautiful, although she would never believe me when I told her—she truly is one of the most beautiful women I know, inside and out. My dad is dressed up also, having swapped his standard uniform of jeans, a T-shirt, and tennis shoes for tan khakis and a light cream polo shirt. My parents are the cutest couple, always holding hands and telling each other of their devotion—like two teenagers except more practical. The new clothes showcase a new side and it is wonderful to see.

I'm so ecstatic at seeing them here at our house that I keep hugging them. Only hours ago, I was bereft at the thought of not having seen them in such a long time and waiting to see them; now, they are in front of me. I have so much to tell them. For now, a warm, happy greeting will have to suffice.

Laughing at my inability to let go, my mom says, "Well, you will never believe it. I finally convinced your father that we should take that cross-country road trip we have been planning for years. After you and Gino said you were leaving for Italy, we decided it was time for us to do something, too."

"You guys inspired us," says my dad.

"We've had such a great time," my mom adds. "The best part is having no schedule. It has been so freeing and liberating. We have not had this much fun in years. I will tell you more about it later, but as we got closer to Virginia, we called Jane to see if she knew when you guys would be back. When she said you were flying in today, well, we had to be here!"

"Mom, Dad, I have been thinking of you so much. I am so happy to see you. This is perfect. I've been planning to get together because we have so much to tell you. I can't believe you are here! This is great!"

Jane says, "There is one more surprise, too. Your mom thought it would be great to call Gino's parents and have them come out. They ran into some traffic, but they should be arriving any time now. You had mentioned a while back you were hoping to get your families together again before the end of summer. We thought this would be a surprise for you."

"I can't think of a better surprise. I love it. Everyone I have been missing so much is here. Thank you so much."

Exchanging hugs and kisses, we usher everyone toward the house. It feels so good to be home. In some ways it feels as if we have been gone forever, and in other ways it's as if we never left. I missed the bluish-purple hydrangeas on full display under the front windows. I missed the pink roses that line the path to the front door. I missed this house, where we created a life together and shared our families, where we welcomed new friends and are now creating our future. It will now be the steppingstone to the next chapter of our lives.

My mom and I walk arm in arm to the front door. The windows have been opened, and the curtains are billowing inside from the slight breeze. I hear music. It's muffled, but I can hear it well enough to know that it is Italian, and it is already having a nostalgic effect on me. When we reach the door, I inhale and breathe in the aroma of garlic. It is as if we are still in Italy, where the smell of garlic was everywhere we went, lingering and always making us hungry.

"Mmm, wow, someone has been busy! It smells so delicious." Jane, the kids, and Luigi follow us inside. Last, the men, having grabbed our luggage from the car, come in and drop our bags in the foyer.

To our surprise, a spread of appetizers rests on the coffee table, and the dining room table is set. Suddenly I realize how hungry I am. Neither of us had much of an appetite on the plane. I pick a black olive from the appetizer tray and pop it into my mouth. Its bittersweetness is divine. As I turn around, Charlie places a glass of red wine in my hand. "This looks amazing. I feel like I am still in Italy! Jane, you didn't have to go to all this trouble."

"Please. It's no big deal. We figured you would be hungry. Your mom and dad prepared the wine and appetizers. Pasta is so easy. Charlie made the salad, and the kids set the table. We stocked you up with a few groceries for breakfast tomorrow, too. Besides, we are all dying to hear about your trip!"

We all gather in the living room, enjoying the appetizers and wine. Gino and I relay the story of our trip, starting from the beginning. It is so good to be with friends and family and hear the kids chattering and playing with Luigi. It is great to be home.

We go on about the museums, the food, the music, the hotel—but mostly we talk about how we found our peace together. The trip healed wounds we didn't know we had and filled us with newfound love: love for each other and life.

About an hour later, filled with the appetizers and relaxed by the wine, we hear the doorbell ring. Gino jumps up from the couch and goes to the front door.

I follow Gino, and we give a warm welcome to his parents. Gino's dad, Antonio, reminds me of an Italian opera singer: handsome and tall and a has deep baritone voice that sounds like he is singing notes when he speaks. He always has a smile on his face, and his warm embrace is so inviting. I can see where Gino gets his charm.

Gino's mom, Evelina, is elegant and beautiful. She has a rhythmic sway when she walks, and like her husband, smiles easily and often. Her presence alone is comforting, and I can see Gino's resemblance to her as well.

"Come in, come in," we say as everyone peeks into the foyer. As Gino leads us into the living room, my dad heads out behind us to help Gino's dad bring their luggage inside.

Over the last year, I have done a lot of self-reflection and made a point to be aware of my surroundings. I try not to let my happiness hinge on material things. I let the people around me fill my life with meaning and purpose. I have learned a lot about being more present and aware of my situation, and this is another one of those instances where I can stand back and look at the fullness of my life and all that surrounds me. A year ago, that would have felt impossible. The heaviness that weighed on my mind, the emptiness that left me depleted, and the constant struggle to make it through each moment, let alone each day, had sucked the life out of me. It was hard to imagine that I would ever feel normal again or that eventually my life would fall back into a meaningful rhythm. It was a struggle that I would not care to repeat and would not wish on anyone. But I know where I have been, and I know now where I am going. I pushed myself even when I did not think I had it in me. I took life one step—one inhale, one exhale—at a time.

Looking around our living room now, I feel as if I am having an out-of-body experience. I think how truly lucky I am to have the salvation of my friends and family. The most important people in my life are standing here with me. They have come to help us celebrate, and I am only too happy to be in a state of mind to participate.

Jane ushers us into the dining room, shaking me out of my nostalgic thoughts. For once, I am taking the opportunity to enjoy the company and not worry about the duties of being a hostess. I am grateful to Jane.

As everyone takes their seats around the table and everyone fills their plates, I keep thinking about how great it is to be home and among my family.

Jane says, "I know you have had plenty of Italian food lately, but we thought you wouldn't mind a little more. I'd like to toast the end of your vacation. It sounds like you had an incredible time, and what better way to end it than a dinner with family and friends? We are so happy to have you both back. To family," Jane says as the adults lift their wine-filled glasses, and the kids raise their glasses of milk. Gino and I exchange a private glance as glasses clink. With happiness all around, we dig into the feast laid out before us.

Later in the evening, after the kitchen is clean and Jane and her family have departed, we begin to feel the toll of the long day. Gino and our dads sit in the living room talking. Evelina and I steal glances at them and cannot help but laugh as all three of their heads droop to one side and then the other as they try to stay awake. Mom, Evelina, and I are also tired from all the excitement and traveling. We soon call it a night and agree to start fresh in the morning. Tomorrow is a new day.

After making sure our parents were comfortable in their bedrooms, I join Gino in our bedroom and find him already sound asleep. I can tell he tried to stay awake, but exhaustion has gotten the better of him. He looks so peaceful.

It feels so good to be home, and the thought of a nice shower and our bed sounds even better. By the time I make it to bed an hour later, drowsiness begins to take over in force. Thinking my last thoughts of the day, I relax in my comfortable surroundings and quickly fade into a deep sleep.

CHAPTER 19

I GET UP EARLY the following morning before the sun is up. Gino is still sleeping beside me, but Luigi is immediately by my side. He must have a radar; he knows my every move before I make it. I put on my robe, and we head to the stairs. Before I make it to the landing, I catch the pleasant aroma of fresh coffee brewing and the chatter of female voices. I find my mom and Evelina in the kitchen. "The coffee smells great," I say. "Good morning! You both are up early." Evelina, wrapped in a green kimono-style robe, is at the counter mixing batter for a sausage quiche. My mom is wearing the pink flowered bathrobe I got her several years ago, and she is baking something too.

I make my way over to Evelina and give her a kiss on the cheek as I walk over to my mom. I kiss my mom on the cheek and peek at what she is preparing. "Is that what I think it is?"

"Good morning, hon. It is. I know cinnamon rolls are your favorite. Your father and I have been on the road for so long, it feels good to do a little baking in an actual kitchen. How are you? You guys were so exhausted. Did you sleep well?"

"Yeah, I slept hard. I was so tired but in a good way. When I woke up, there was so much on my mind that I couldn't get back to sleep. I figured I would get up rather than lie there and think."

I watch my mom and Evelina bustling around the kitchen. The rolls are rising; soon the kitchen will be smelling of cinnamon. My mom is washing a few mixing bowls while Evelina finishes the sausage quiche and places it in the oven. I pour myself a coffee and sit at the kitchen table as Evelina joins me.

"So, what will you and Dad do next? How far are you going before you head home?"

"Oh, I don't know. We don't have any set plans. I think that's why we enjoyed this trip so much. This is the first time we've made a trip like this. We never thought of traveling without an agenda until you said you and Gino were doing it. You know how your father likes to have everything planned. And we've never gone away for more than a week or two. But we've been on the road for over three weeks now, driving when we want and stopping when we want, and he's been terrific. It was an adjustment, but he has learned to enjoy it. The best part is that he can work from the road, so it's not like we have to rush home. We should have done this years ago. I'm enjoying every minute."

Forty-five minutes later, the timer on the oven beeps and Evelina gets up to take the quiche out of the oven. Evelina sits to join me. As I'm watching my mom, she opens the oven and places the cinnamon rolls inside, then sets the timer. She looks so happy. She looks radiant. After pouring herself some coffee, she joins us at the table.

"So," my mom says, "I think the men will be sleeping for a while. Was the trip everything you were hoping for?"

"Oh, Mom, Evelina, it was fantastic. I think it was the best thing we could have done. I've had such a hard time this past year, as you both know. I haven't snapped out of it as easily as I have in years past. I felt like I was drowning. But I think both of us realized that for the last several years, we have been . . . well, stuck. Don't get me wrong, Gino and I are great. It's just that . . . well . . . to be honest, I think Gino has been hiding his discontent as well. The thing is, with him, I don't think he even knew it."

Evelina gets up to pour another cup of coffee and then brings the pot over to fill our cups. "Yes, Gino was like that as a child, too. Perhaps he has never learned to listen to his feelings. I suppose sometimes that's good, but sometimes you need to hear yourself. It's easy to get lost and not know it," she says as she sets the coffee pot back onto the hot plate and comes back to join us.

I take a sip of coffee and sit back in my chair. I breathe in the smell of the cinnamon rolls baking and continue, "It was like waking up every morning in a beautiful painting come to life. The rich colors of the buildings, the sounds of the water, the boats and ships, the smell of bread and garlic—oh, it was wonderful! You should have seen the view from our balcony. It was magnificent. And our hotel! I was happy just admiring our room, but the lobby was like a museum gallery."

My mom, smiling and cradling her coffee the way I do, says, "I love your hair, by the way. The style suits you. You looked beautiful when we saw you at Thanksgiving, too—you always do—but you also lacked the glow you always seem to have about you. It's back. Whatever you guys were looking for while you were there, you must have found it."

Sitting at the table deep in conversation, the timer beeps for the cinnamon rolls. As my mom gets up to take them out of the oven, I continue telling them more about our trip. She listens intently as she starts making the icing to go on top of the rolls and stops me every so often to ask a question.

After almost an hour of relaying our trip with all the charming details to paint her the perfect picture in her mind so she could remember when she visited fifteen years before and for Evelina to rekindle her old memories of living there, I start telling them about my book.

"Do you remember after my senior year of college when my friends and I went to Italy?"

"Of course!" my mom laughs. "How could I forget? You called us to tell us to hurry and pack and come to Italy because you were getting married. Your father and I were so shocked, having not met Gino yet. I was so happy we had our passports!"

Evelina chimes in, "We were so surprised too because Gino has always said since he was a kid he wasn't going to get married. When he called to ask us to come, we knew it had to be something special."

"Well, during that time I kept a journal of all the things we did, the sights, the food, the concerts, the touristy things. I didn't want to forget anything. And then, of course, how I met Gino. As time went on, I forgot about it. Anyway, last summer, I stumbled upon that journal. I hadn't seen it in nearly fifteen years. For fun, I started typing, turning some notes and fragments into paragraphs. It turned into quite a few pages. Jane asked me about it, and one thing led to another. Her publishing company wants to publish my book!"

"You wrote a book? That's fantastic, Fran!"

"Wow, that's wonderful," my mom says as she refills our coffee mugs that have quietly drained and places some rolls onto a plate to set them on the table. "So, what is the next step?"

"Well, I just completed the manuscript. I still have a few touch-ups, but it's mostly done. I told Jane I would have it to her shortly. I need time to focus on our new plans."

"There's more?"

"Well, now that I'm writing more and helping Gino in the shop, I want him to do what he loves, too."

"Isn't he doing that?"

"Well, yes, but he loves to build boats, and he's been building everything but that. So we've talked extensively and decided on a plan. We've lived here for a long time, but nothing has to hold us here. We decided it's time to make a change. We are moving!"

"What? When?"

"Yeah, I know. We never considered it before, but after this trip we had lots to talk about. It's time. We need to move on. Fortunately, we are both able to do that together. We can open a shop somewhere else. Why not do it closer to the water? Gino can build boats. I can help run the shop and write. It's perfect."

Unable to resist any longer, I grab a plate off the table and take a cinnamon roll. Everyone knows I love sweets, but my favorite part is taking that first bite of a cinnamon roll. Breathing in the aroma, feeling the stickiness of the cooled icing on my lips, and savoring that first bite of pure sweetness brings me so much delight. I close my eyes and let all my taste buds enjoy the deliciousness of the breakfast sweet. When I open my eyes again, I see my mom and Evelina laughing at me. It's completely worth every calorie, I tell myself. Yes, I've been splurging a lot lately, but I will get back on track soon. Besides, how often do I enjoy a special treat with my mom and Evelina?

Gino, Antonio, and my dad walk into the kitchen as if pulled out of their beds by the smell of the cinnamon rolls.

"Morning, everyone," I say. "Dad, I hear you guys have been having a wonderful time on your trip. I think it's fabulous you are doing this."

"That's what your mom says," he replies as he squeezes her shoulders and bends over to give her a kiss. "I have to admit it's nice not having to plan anything."

Pulling out the other three kitchen chairs, the men sit with us and dig into the rolls and the sausage quiche Evelina places on the table.

"Graham," my mother says, "your daughter and son-in-law have some pretty exciting news to share."

"Oh?" Dad says.

I smile at Gino and say, "We are moving."

"Moving? You guys haven't lived here that long, have you?"

"Dad, we've been here fifteen years."

"Really? It's been that long? Time sure flies. I guess your mom was right about us taking this trip. So, when are you moving and where?"

"Well, we have a lot to work out before we sell. We've only been working on this for a week."

We spend the rest of the morning drinking coffee and discussing plans. It is another one of those perfect moments filled with joyful commotion: The voices of our fathers as they sit talking together; our mothers strategizing about the packing for our eventual move; Luigi running around by the door waiting to go out. The smell of breakfast is in the air; the coffee maker is gurgling again as one more pot has just been made. I catch Gino's eye, and he gives me a wink. Yes, I'm going to miss this place. It is where we all became a family. But I am ready to move on. We are ready. It is time. With so much change on the horizon, I cannot contain my excitement. Every day is something new, and the anticipation is joyous.

CHAPTER 20

It has been several weeks since we got back from Italy. Luigi got back to his usual rhythm without missing a beat. As I let him out this morning and watch him run around, I am again thankful that our long time away didn't cause him any harm.

Gino left for the shop early this morning to get a jump on a few things. I want to look through my pages before I send the final draft to Jane.

Hearing the coffee perking that I started earlier, I pull out my laptop from my leather travel bag sitting on one of the dining chairs in the kitchen and set it up on the table. Taking a seat in front of it, I let my fingers begin typing away as if some magical force takes over. I have looked forward to this feeling and am coming up with all sorts of ideas to write about to keep my mind in this fantastic awakening. With my hands on the keyboard, I let my fingers glide easily over the keys with additions and edits that come so causally as if I am playing an instrument and the sound is effortlessly filling up the room. The ideas flood through my mind faster than I can type and it is hard to keep up. By the time I finish, I feel my heart racing at the pure satisfaction of knowing I have completed my marathon. I only worked for about an hour because it was still dark when I came downstairs this morning.

Satisfied and flying high, realizing I am done, I get up from the table, pull a mug from the kitchen cabinet, and fill it with coffee. Inhaling the freshly brewed aroma nestled between my hands, I slowly begin looking around the room and realize that it will not be ours for much longer. How many mornings have I sat at this table and cried over the years, over this past year? How often have I used this phone with no Caller ID because I love it? How often have we had parties and entertained with friends and family over the holidays? How many conversations have Gino and I had in this kitchen while making weekend brunches or weekday dinners? While I will miss this house and appreciate all the love, comfort, and security we have found here over the last fifteen years, I am ready to move on. It is time to take point of my life instead of letting the paralysis and quicksand that so easily ruled my world for so long enough take hold.

Stepping outside to join Luigi, I can see slivers of sun breaking beyond the horizon. It is a perfect August morning. The humidity and steaminess we usually encounter this time of year have abated over the last few days. Instead, it has been replaced with a gentle breeze whispering against my skin. The effect is like a feather, slowly tickling up and down my arm. Sitting in one of the two old sun-faded wicker chairs on the patio, I commit the daybreak to memory, sip my coffee, admire the beautiful sunrise, and relinquish all my thoughts. I know it is going to be a beautiful day. I know it will be because I am going to personally make it a beautiful day.

Gino and I had gotten used to the laid-back mentality of the locals when we were in Italy, and we've tried hard to keep the same feeling alive here as well. Other than Gino working at the shop, we have managed to transition well into blending our lifestyle with the one we left several weeks back. While we certainly have our obligations and commitments to attend to, they do not rule our lives like they had in the past. The enjoyment of everyday occurrences has become something we relish together. Sitting at the start of the evening to enjoy a glass of wine to celebrate our day, playing a game of cards together in the evening instead of watching television, swaying in unison to the beat of the soft dinner music that is playing on an old record player as we prepare dinner, but mostly spending cherished time together that feels more fulfilling than spending our evenings alone and separated by work or mindless other activities of no importance.

The day flew by fast. It's almost five in the afternoon and Gino called earlier to say he was going to be late but should be home around eight. It was perfect timing when the doorbell rang. Wondering who it might be, I head to the door to open it.

"Hey Jane," I said so excitedly. "Come on in."

"I'm not interrupting anything, am I?"

"No, absolutely not. Gino is going to be late. I was getting ready to sit out on the patio. Want to join me?"

"That sounds great. Charlie is picking up the kids and I happen to be in the area. I wasn't sure if you were home, but I wanted to stop by and say hi. I figured I better now that I can since I won't have too many more opportunities."

"I'm so glad you did. How about some wine? I have a bottle of cabernet I was going to open," I say as we walk to the kitchen.

"Definitely. I can use a glass. I love my family, but it is nice to have a few moments away to breathe and unwind. I feel like I have been going non-stop for months now and can't catch up."

"You came to the right place," I say as I pull out two wine glasses from the top shelf of the kitchen cabinet and open a bottle of cabernet sauvignon. Pouring two glasses of the cabernet, I hand one glass to Jane. I have been slowly going thru the cabinets to get rid of things we don't need and in doing so I found this lovely wooden tray. I always loved it, but I forgot all about it and if I don't see it, I don't use it. Excited to have an opportunity to use it now, I grab a bowl of grapes and a block of Swiss cheese from the fridge and place them all along with the bottle of wine and a knife on the tray, we head out onto the back patio with Luigi to enjoy the early summer evening.

We clink our glasses together in a toast to celebrate each other and our friendship, and taking our first sip, we each sit back in the weathered and unattractive wicker chairs that I had sat in earlier this morning. Making a mental note, I tell myself that when we move, these chairs won't be making the journey.

"This is good wine. I love the taste of it. Charlie and I have been experimenting with new wines recently. We've been trying to describe the taste so we can become more accomplished wine drinkers," Jane says with a laugh. "This tastes of blackberries and currants."

Reaching for the bottle, I look at the description and confirm that she is right. "Very good. Your work is paying off."

"We figured we both like wine so much maybe we should perfect our palates," Jane says, smiling and holding out the glass of wine as she examines it in the air against the beautiful setting sun. "We are picking hobbies that we both like to explore together. So far, it's been good. We've gone to a few tastings and met some new people. We've had more to talk about besides the kids. It's refreshing to feel like we have more in common and things to talk about. Kind of feels like we are dating again, and to think we just had a baby."

"I get it. Gino and I have been the same way until recently. We got so comfortable that that feeling you get being in a new relationship had gone away. It's not that I didn't have those exciting feelings because I always do, but we got so complacent, I guess. It's nice to be interested in things together."

"So tell me, how is your book coming along?"

"Well, I have some news for you! I'm done. I completed it this morning. Officially, it is all yours. I can't wait to hear what you think of it," I say, taking a sip of wine and letting the taste linger in my mouth before swallowing and feeling the remains of it on my lips.

"Has Gino read it yet?"

"No, he asked me, but I told him I wanted to wait for him to read it until it was completed."

"Can you send it tomorrow? We can get going on it and maybe they can have it in print by the new year."

"Yeah, absolutely. I can't believe it's done."

Popping a grape into my mouth and letting the flavor burst open, I look up at the sky, tilting my head back against the chair. As I sink my teeth down, I can feel the sweetness surrounding my taste buds. It is a taste so delicious it reminds me of when I was a kid. I loved grapes and would eat so many of them that the juice would spill from my cheeks.

"This has been such a beautiful summer, one of the best years I have had since I can remember. I would never have predicted this is how it would go. I honestly dreaded this year. You know everything is such a whirlwind around the holidays. I always loved January. I saw it as a fresh, clean start. But the beginning of this year was different. It almost seemed like by the time January came around, I was afraid to start the year. I knew it was going to be a letdown and I was not sure how I wasn't going to cope with it. But then when Gino and I came up with our plan, I felt better. And then I owe so much to you. I'm so grateful to you, Jane."

"Me? I didn't do anything. You did all the work."

"Yes, but you urged me to let you see it. If you hadn't, I might never have finished it, let alone tried to get it published. I feel like now I have so much to look forward to. I feel so many possibilities."

"You did this all yourself. You should be proud. I know we all are."

Taking one last sip of wine, Jane sets down her empty glass and looks at her watch. Standing up, she says, "I'd better get going before it gets too late. Charlie will be wondering where I am."

"Did I tell you what a wonderful friend I have?" Smiling, I walk with Jane to the front door, and we say our goodbyes, promising to get in touch in a few days, knowing our time is limited because of the pending move.

By the time Jane left, it was close to eight and Gino should be home soon. I had gone outside to watch the sky transition from a beautiful baby blue to the soft colors of cotton candy pink sprinkled with oranges and reds. It is an awesome wonder to watch the rise and set of the sun. The same routine happens every day, yet most of us never realize it. It is a wonderment that few of us take the time to witness the magnificent event. I started the day in this very spot watching the sunrise. Somehow it seemed fitting to close the day by admiring the sunset in its tremendous glory.

Watching the setting sun, I dozed off because unexpectedly I hear the click of the outside patio door open and close, and I can see fireflies off in the distance.

"Hey, babe. Wow, it is a beautiful night. I'm a little later than I thought. I know we were going to decide on dinner when I got home, but since it got to be so late, I swung by Ruby's and got some cheeseburgers and fries instead. I would have gotten milkshakes, too, but I didn't think they would last the ride home."

"Oh, that smells wonderful. I wasn't super hungry until I smelled the burgers. I've got some wine open. Do you want a glass of wine or a beer?"

"I'll take a beer. Stay here, I'll get it. I'll grab some ketchup and napkins too."

As Gino goes back inside, I pull two chairs together and light some tea candles I had brought out earlier. They make us look as if we're in a fairytale. I love this kind of summer night—where you leave the worries and stressors of the day at the door the moment you cross the threshold, and everything outside your home is waiting for tomorrow.

Walking back outside and sitting in the chair next to me, Gino pulls out the burgers and fries from the bag. The to-go boxes that the food comes in kept the burgers hot and taking off the lid, I can see the steam travel up and smell the deliciousness of the fries.

"My mouth is watering. This looks so good," I say, taking a bite and letting the burger and tomato juice run down my cheeks. Taking a napkin and wiping my face, I sit back on the chair and reach for my wine. "What a perfect night."

"As excited and as ready as I am to go, I will miss this. I never thought the time would come."

"I know. Me too. I guess we get so wrapped up in things and time passes. I think it's good for us. No, I think it's great for us. I'm excited that we are making this happen. It's all because of you, Fran."

"I think it's because of us. We needed to find our way. Fortunately, we are together. Gino, I can't tell you how excited I am. I like the more personal discussions we've been having this past year. I like talking to you about anything. I've always known that I can, but it's different now; I think things have changed. I am excited for you to read my book. I think it will tell you a lot of things that I always wanted to tell you but never did. I never knew how."

Taking a sip of wine and placing it on the table, I look at Gino. "I think the book was always meant to be. I think it's the reason I was supposed to write it. I finally feel like I'm in a good place."

Gino reaches across the table and takes my hand. "I'm so proud of you. We are starting a new chapter together, and I have the feeling that it will be even better this time around."

August turns to September rather quickly, and before we know it, October greets us with falling leaves and the smell of open pit fires on cool evenings. Even though we are busy, we take the time to mark the changes of the seasons. Gone are the days of rushing around, leaving the house before sunrise and coming home after sunset. We have made a pact to fully embrace every moment and witness the beauty bestowed upon us. It's easy to get wrapped up in the day-to-day and miss the simple moments in front of us. I've missed too many over the years, and I'm fully aware of how much these moments mean to me. The beauty is not just in those fleeting moments in time; it is the collection of those moments that has the awesome ability to last a lifetime. If we are wise, we learn to deeply appreciate the sensational peaks of the seasons, which, after all, are granted to us but once a year.

I know I tell myself repeatedly how far we have come, but I keep having to remind myself where I was a year ago. It is easy to look back and see the sequence of events that led us to where we are now. They were the instigators that made us open our eyes and realize our potential, my potential. But at the time, it was so painful, and the possibilities were invisible. In my heart, I know I need to recognize there is always potential.

Now more than ever, I have dreams and possibilities ahead of me, and the thought of pursuing them together with Gino keeps my spirits soaring.

It's been years since I have felt this good. I can't honestly recall ever having felt this good. I suspect I've always been prone to spirals of negative thoughts, but it was not until recently that I knew how bad it could get. There were plenty of days, too many to count, when I didn't think I could get out of bed, let alone have the energy to talk. The poison in my mind percolated throughout my body as if I was perpetually sick with the flu. My body ached, my mind was numb, and the thought of being around people drained whatever energy I could produce. Surrounding myself with those closest to me—my friends and family—was a lifesaver. They unknowingly gave me the will to pick myself up and keep moving forward.

For that, I am eternally grateful. I'm not sure they will ever know how their presence, support, and love have affected me.

More than ever, I am mindful of my feelings and how good feelings are strengthened when I share them with others. My feelings of happiness multiply abundantly when I am with Gino, when I feel inspired, when I feel excited, when I have hope, when I have purpose, and most of all when I see the possibilities of what lies ahead.

Perhaps this realization comes with age, or perhaps it is a lesson learned through years of silent suffering—but I have found that the people I love are a lighthouse constantly sending out that glimmer of hope. Knowing that there are people on the other end of that flashing light who will always be there for me, now more than ever, I want to cling to my life raft and make it to shore. Now that I figured out the enigma to unlock the key to a life flowing with joy and wonder, the idea of hope and possibilities is enough to pull me through.

As luck would have it, on one beautiful autumn day, the prospect of turning our dream into reality became certain. With our car packed in the driveway and Gino sitting in the driver's seat, I stood on the front stoop, taking one last look at the beautiful backdrop of what was only moments ago our house, the place where we spent the last fifteen years. Memories flooded my mind in a flash as if reliving every second of those years in a mere moment of reflection. Having closed the door to that chapter, I am more than ready to start creating the next chapter, one step, one breath, one day at a time. And when I worry about what will come next, I think to myself not to fear. This is a life in progress.

ABOUT THE AUTHOR

Originally from Springfield, Virginia, Michelle Fornelli lived with her family overseas until relocating back to Northern Virginia at a young age. After graduating from Mary Baldwin University, she followed in her father's footsteps and commissioned into the United States Army where she also served overseas. Following her military commitment, she explored fun-filled career opportunities that formed new paths and friendships along the way. For the last fifteen years, she has been a proponent of holistic and complimentary therapies and is a licensed massage therapist. She and her husband live in Fauquier County, Virginia with their pup, Henri.

www.ingramcontent.com/pod-product-compliance
Lightning Source LLC
Chambersburg PA
CBHW030957210726
48290CB00007B/2350